KATHERIN

The
ONE AND
ON

illustrated by
Patricia Castelao

LY

RUBY

HARPER
An Imprint of HarperCollins*Publishers*

Library of Congress Control Number: 2023930013
ISBN 978-0-06-308008-9 (trade bdg.) — ISBN 978-0-06-333826-5 (int.)
ISBN 978-0-06-331811-3 (special ed.) — ISBN 978-0-06-333926-2 (special ed.)

Typography by Sarah Piersen
23 24 25 26 27 LBC 5 4 3 2 1

First Edition

for all the
elephants alone

and for

Tara Weikum,
with endless thanks

If anyone wants to know what elephants are like,
they are like people, only more so.
—Pierre Corneille

elephant body language

watch out!

I'm scared

let's play

we're pals

I'm worried

I'm silly

elephant glossary

aunt: (I) the sister of your father or mother; (2) term of affection used by elephants when addressing a female herd member

calf: the young of certain mammals, including cows, whales, and elephants

the Creed of the Herd: a belief passed down through elephant generations that states, "An elephant alone is not an elephant."

drought: an extended period without rain

dung: manure

dust bathing: covering the body with a layer of fine dirt to protect the skin from the sun and parasites, either by rolling on the ground or tossing dust with the trunk

ear-flaps: rapid movement of the ears, often as part of greeting, bonding, or excitement. Ear-flapping can also be used to signal aggression or for heat regulation.

elebrella: shade provided to an elephant calf by the belly or shadow of an adult elephant

floppy-run: moving with a relaxed, easy stride

the Four Lodestars: a set of four principles—kindness, wonder, courage, and gratitude—that elephants use to guide their conduct

matriarch: the female leader of a family or group

mudfun: wallowing in soft, wet earth *(informal; see also:* **pondplay***)*

Not Okay Behavior: inappropriate conduct

oops-oopsie: elephant game involving water spray from trunks

pondplay: fun and games in a small body of water

savanna (African): biodiverse ecosystem featuring huge grasslands with scattered trees

sentinel: a guardian or protector

slapsplash: deliberately hitting water with your trunk (*informal; see also:* **pondplay**)

trunk: the long, movable snout of an elephant

trunk-boost: lifting or nudging another elephant; usually, an adult assisting a calf

trunk-trudge: to walk slowly or dawdle, often dragging your trunk

Tuskday: traditional celebration after the arrival of a young elephant's tusks

Tusky: nickname for young elephants just after their tusks appear

my big little problem

Nobody ever listens to the littlest elephant.

And around here, the littlest elephant is me.

brave

When you're the littlest elephant, even if you very help-fully say, "Hey, I'd better jump in the pond to see if any giant hungry snaggletoothed crocodiles might be hid-ing in there," one of the grown-ups will say, "I think you've had plenty of water play today."

And then if you slapsplash the muddy water with your trunk just to be *extra* sure there aren't actually any giant hungry snaggletoothed crocodiles hiding in there because you are that amazingly brave, not that anyone appreciates you, another grown-up will loop her trunk around your tummy and pull you away from the water's edge and say, "Come on, silly Tusky."

That's a real for instance.

Also, when you're the littlest elephant, they call you things like "Tusky."

I'm going to ask my family not to call me that anymore, because I think it's teasing and teasing is a Not Okay Behavior.

And besides, my name is Ruby.

My aunt Akello says it's elephant tradition to call little elephants "Tusky" when their tusks first appear. She says it's like "Buttercup" or "Ru-Ru" or "Twizzle-trunk" or any of the other gazillion nicknames they have for me.

But I don't like "Tusky."

I don't like it because I have a secret I can't tell the other elephants.

don't tell anyone

My secret is that I hate my tusks.

all about tusks

In case you're not an elephant, here is what you need to know about tusks.

Tusks are kind of like teeth, which you probably have unless you are an anteater or a turtle or an earthworm. Regular elephant teeth are flat, not pointy, and good for chomping things like grass until it gets nice and smushy. We grow six new sets of teeth in our lives, I guess because we use them so much.

But nobody cares about those teeth. It's our tusks everyone is interested in.

Especially humans.

Tusks are the white pointy things that extend from the sides of our mouths like big front teeth that forgot to stop growing. They are hard and smooth and curved like new moons. Lots of elephants like me, the ones who come from Africa, grow tusks. Boys and girls.

Elephants use our tusks for all kinds of things. They help with eating and digging and playing and sometimes even fighting. They are so important that when your tusks arrive, elephants hold a special ceremony to celebrate the occasion.

Elephants love any excuse for a party.

Aunt Akello says tusks are a sign you're growing up. She says the ceremony is a way of honoring that passage.

On my Tuskday I have to give a speech while the other elephants listen.

It's like a birthday party, only without the fun.

protesting

The reason the grown-ups made me get out of the pond is because it's time for me to practice for my ceremony. But my actual Tuskday is two whole days from now, so I don't see why I couldn't have had maybe just five more minutes of mudfun.

Especially since the pond mud is extra gooey this time of year.

Anyway, I'm hiding behind this tree because I don't want to practice. In case you're wondering.

I'm not pouting. I'm protesting.

Unfortunately, it's hard to hide all of you when you're an elephant. Even a little elephant is big compared to a bug or a squirrel or a kid.

hide-and-seek

Yesterday, I tried hiding behind a different tree when T.J., one of the park veterinarians, wanted to check my new tusks.

She found me pretty quick.

I need better hiding places.

why

Aunt Akello is heading this way. There are six elephants in our little herd, and Aunt Akello is the matriarch, which means she is the boss of us. An elephant matriarch is like a teacher and a counselor and a rescuer and a yeller and a helper and a nudger and a guider all rolled into one.

I hope she isn't mad. I really do try to listen to the grown-ups, but every now and then my ears misbehave.

Aunt Akello says someday I'll outgrow this stage.

Aunt Akello sighs a lot.

My aunt Laheli, who'd been scratching her back on a nearby tree, lopes over and taps me with her trunk. Aunt Laheli is my youngest aunt, and she loves mud almost as much as I do. Also she likes to play oops-oopsie, which is when you spray someone with water from your trunk and say, "Oops!" and then they get to spray you back twice as long and say, "Oopsie!" But only if they want to play the game, because otherwise that is another Not Okay Behavior.

An awful lot of things are Not Okay Behaviors. Somebody really ought to make a list.

Just for a day, I would like to make all the rules. A good one would be Play in the Mud as Long as You Want Even If It's Way Past Your Bedtime.

"You know Akello can see you behind that tree, Tusky," Aunt Laheli says.

"I don't want to practice for the ceremony," I say. "Also I don't want to celebrate my Tuskday. Also please don't call me Tusky."

Aunt Laheli cocks her head. Her right eye is golden and large and always smiley. Her left eye is white and blank and doesn't work anymore. A man at the roadside zoo where she used to live poked it with a stick.

"But your Tuskday is a big deal," she says. She lowers her head so I can see how grand her tusks are. They practically glow in the sunlight, and they're a little bit swirly at the tips, which is a nice touch.

"I just don't care about my Tuskday," I say.

"Is it because your tusks still hurt?" she asks. "'Cause that goes away pretty fast, I promise."

"They don't hurt anymore," I say. "That's not why I don't want to celebrate."

I can tell by Aunt Laheli's expression that she doesn't exactly understand me.

I'd try to explain, but I don't exactly understand me, either.

good advice

When your tusks start growing at around age two, it hurts.

Like the world's biggest toothache.

When my tusks first poked out, my five aunts had plenty of advice for me.

Aunt Masika said, "Rub the sore spots on a mossy log and count to fifty-three."

Aunt Laheli said, "Put your head under ice-cold water and blow teeny-tiny bubbles."

Aunt Elodie said, "Eat a sour apple with at least two worms in it."

Aunt Zaina said, "Take a nap in the sun, but whatever you do, be sure not to snore."

Then there was Aunt Akello's advice.

She just looked at me and said, "Don't think about it."

You try having two giant pointy teeth pop out of your face and see how long you stop thinking about it.

lucky

I love my aunts lots. Even though sometimes they can be bossy or grumpy or full of weird advice.

Lucky for me, I also have two uncles.

My uncle Ivan is a gorilla.

My uncle Bob is a dog.

Families can be complicated.

another complication

When I was a baby, I had a mom, too. I guess that's true of most babies.

I don't have her anymore.

I haven't had much luck when it comes to moms.

the best

I don't know where I would be right now without Uncle
Ivan and Uncle Bob.

Those two guys, and my aunt Stella, an old elephant,
changed my life forever. Especially Aunt Stella, who
loved me when I most needed to be loved.

The four of us met a long time ago at a place called the
Exit 8 Big Top Mall and Video Arcade.

Aunt Stella and I shared a cage. So did Uncle Ivan and
Uncle Bob. (Even though Uncle Bob could come and
go as he pleased, he slept every night on Uncle Ivan's
big, warm tummy.)

If anyone ever asks you if you'd like to live in a cage in
a shopping mall, the answer is no.

lost

While we were at the mall, we lost Aunt Stella.

Uncle Ivan prefers to say that she "passed on."

Uncle Bob just says she "died."

But I always say we lost her. Because that's how it feels. Like if I just look long enough, I'll find her again.

I miss her so much. Sometimes it hurts like a thousand new tusks all at once.

the park

We don't live at the mall anymore.

Where Uncle Ivan and I live now has a long name: Wildworld Zoological Park and Sanctuary. But everybody just calls it "the park" because otherwise there are way too many words.

I live in Elephant Odyssey. Uncle Ivan lives in Gorilla World. We are next-door neighbors.

After that come other animal lands. They are separated with fences and walls and ponds and pathways. That way nobody eats anybody.

Uncle Bob lives nearby, in a house a few blocks from here. He shares it with our friend Julia and her parents and Bob's sister, Boss, and his nephew, Rowdy. Also two guinea pigs named Minnie and Moo.

Before the park, I lived at the shopping mall. But I was born in Africa.

I've had many homes. I've even had many names.

Uncle Ivan likes to say that for a little elephant, I am very well traveled. Then Uncle Bob says, "Good thing you always have your trunk, Ruby."

Uncle Bob is a funny guy.

Aunt Akello

Aunt Akello joins me at my not-very-good-for-hiding tree. She is wearing her disappointed face. She has lovely, complicated wrinkles near her eyes.

"Ruby," she says, "I know you don't want to practice for your Tuskday. But it's important, dear one."

Aunt Akello is bigger than my other aunts and older, too. Her skin is ridged like the bark of an ancient oak. Here and there her ears are notched, and her right tusk has a chip in it. When she speaks, it sounds like the noise my feet make when I walk on sand, low and swooshy.

Aunt Akello's voice gets even softer when she is not happy with you. Somehow that makes her even scarier. Which is a pretty neat trick, if you think about it.

I sometimes wonder how she got the big chip in her tusk. But I don't want to ask her in case it is not a nice story.

I know plenty of not-nice stories already.

"I really don't need to practice for my Tuskday," I say. I kick the tree trunk with my right front foot. Gently, because trees are like quiet friends and you have to be kind to them.

"Have you planned what you are going to say?" Aunt Akello asks.

"I'm growing up which is a big deal and I need to be responsible and all that stuff and yay I have tusks." I don't look at her because I can feel a lecture on its way, the way the air gets fizzy when a storm is coming.

She sighs, long and slow. Like I said, Aunt Akello sighs a lot.

"Have you learned the Creed of the Herd?"

"'An elephant alone is not an elephant,'" I say. "But I don't understand what that means and just in case you're wondering, I think this whole thing is kind of silly."

Another sigh from Aunt Akello. "Don't think too hard about the words," she says. "Just feel them."

"But words aren't for feeling," I say. "Words are for hearing and saying and maybe singing. Also yelling and whispering and—"

"Ruby," Aunt Akello interrupts me. "Enough, dear."

"Sorry, Aunt Akello," I say.

My words hang in the air like tired butterflies. I am waiting for Aunt Akello to remind me about Not Okay Behavior, but after a while she lifts her head and points toward the hill where the gorillas live.

"I see Ivan and Bob up there," she says. "Why don't you go and spend some time with them? That's enough for today, Tusky."

I decide to ignore the "Tusky" just this once. Then I wait some more, in case there's a catch. But she gives me a trunk-nudge and even smiles a little.

Elephant smiles are all in their eyes, the way bird smiles are all in their songs.

"Tell them I said hello," says Aunt Akello.

"I will, I promise, and thank you so-so-so much, Aunt Akello," I say extra fast, and I am already running toward the place where I feel safest. Where the ones I love are waiting for me and no one cares about my tusks.

floppy-running

I floppy-run all the way up the hill.

Maybe you don't think of elephants as runners. We probably seem more like trampers or plodders or stompers. But we can run pretty fast when we need to, and we have different kinds of running.

My favorite is called floppy-running.

Floppy-running is the best kind of running because it happens when you are feeling good about the world and like you could almost fly if you weren't an elephant and also had some wings, because they would for sure help.

When you floppy-run, your ears and trunk and tail go wherever they choose. Your legs just kind of float in the air and your feet skip along like they just heard a really good joke.

Watch a baby elephant sometime. They love to floppy-run.

But sometimes grown-ups do it, too.

It is always nice to see grown-ups act silly. They don't do it nearly enough, if you ask me.

Maybe if they floppy-ran more, they wouldn't have such a big list of Not Okay Behaviors.

At the top of the hill, a stone wall separates the gorillas and elephants. There's a small pond on the elephant side, but the mud isn't great there. I like our larger pond, where the mud is just right, nice and slippery. It's like Jell-O, which the keepers sometimes give us for a treat. If Jell-O came in gloopy dark brown.

Anyway, the gorilla area and the elephant area meet like two slices of pie. At the center there's a keepers' shed, along with a big ol' magnolia tree and a bench shaped like a gorilla holding out his arms. It's a hidden place where visitors hardly ever go, and it's perfect for a nice chat with your favorite gorilla and dog.

Bob calls this spot "Canine Corner," 'cause it's the only place in the park where he's allowed.

Julia's dad works at the park, and all the employees know Uncle Bob. They kind of forget to notice that sometimes there's a little dog hiding in Julia's backpack.

I think they let him visit because Uncle Bob and Uncle Ivan have been pals for so long. They need each other the way I need them.

"Ruby, my girl! Got a riddle for me?" Uncle Bob calls as Julia settles him on the stone wall. Uncle Bob is wiry and tiny and fuzzy and brown. He wants the world to think he's tough. But he's a softie at heart.

"I have lots, Uncle Bob!" I call. I love riddles almost as much as I love floppy-running and muddy ponds.

Julia waves to me. "Hi, Ruby!"

I trumpet back and throw my trunk in the air.

Julia laughs. She has a great laugh, sweet and shimmery. Today her long, dark hair is pulled back, and she is wearing a baseball cap with a picture of an elephant on it.

Uncle Ivan is lying on his back near a bush, smelling a pink flower cradled in his palm. Nearby, Aunt Kinyani, his constant companion, is chewing a mango. She is a very energetic eater.

The first time I saw Uncle Ivan, I could not believe how scary and huge he was. A silverback gorilla has the strength of eight humans, and I was just a tiny elephant, after all. But when I looked into Uncle Ivan's eyes and saw the deep pools of kindness there, I knew

I had found a true friend.

"Julia!" Uncle Ivan calls. "I'm so glad you're here!"

"Hi, Uncle Ivan!" I say. I sit near the edge of the pond. "Hi, Aunt Kinyani!"

Aunt Kinyani shakes her head. "My dear, dear Ruby," she says. "How many times do I have to explain to you that you are a pachyderm, not a primate, and therefore not my niece?"

Julia shakes her finger at Uncle Bob. "I'll be back in a few minutes," she says. "No funny business, you."

She always says that to him.

He winks at me. "I can't help being funny."

He always says that, too.

Julia waves goodbye and we watch her head down the path toward her dad's office. George used to work at the mall, but now he has a big job at the park caring for the grounds. The park is huge and full of all kinds of species: mammals and reptiles and birds and fish and amphibians and insects. It's a safe place, and they take good care of us here.

But it's not a perfect place. It's not the wild.

I guess you could say it's our not-quite-home-sweet-home.

a riddle

"So let's hear one of those riddles, Ruby," Uncle Bob says. He pauses to nibble a toenail with his sharp little teeth. "You know I love me a good riddle."

I clear my throat. "What can be as big as an elephant and still weigh nothing?"

Uncle Bob tilts his head. Uncle Ivan taps his chin. "I'll give you a second to think about it," I say. "'Cause this is a tricky one."

"All right, Ruby. Ya got me. I am confused and confounded and confuzzled," Bob says. "What can be as big as an elephant and still weigh nothing?"

I wait before I tell him, because that's how you're supposed to do it.

"Her shadow!" I exclaim.

Everyone laughs, even Aunt Kinyani, who accidentally spits out some of her mango.

"Good one, girl," Uncle Bob says.

"You are the cleverest elephant in the whole wide world," says Uncle Ivan.

Uncle Ivan sometimes gets a little carried away, but I don't mind. I wish everybody could have an Uncle Ivan in their life.

"When I was just born," I say, "elephant shadows meant the world to me. It gets really, really hot in Africa, and

when you're a baby, your skin is very delicate. Right away I learned that hiding under grown-up elephants was a good idea."

"A good idea," Bob points out, "as long as they don't sit down."

"In our herd we had lots of elephants," I say. "So if my mama was busy, I could use one of my aunts or big sisters or my grandmother for an elebrella."

"An elebrella," Ivan repeats. "That would have been very useful during my time in Africa, for sure. Even in the jungle, I remember hiding from the sun at midday."

"'Course, with Aunt Stella at the mall, I didn't need her shadow because we didn't have much sunshine," I add. "But hiding under her I felt safe anyway."

I don't say the other part I'm thinking.

How Aunt Stella's memory is like a different kind of shadow, following me day and night.

quiet

Uncle Ivan and Uncle Bob fall quiet, and I feel bad.

We hardly ever talk about Aunt Stella anymore. We used to. But then one morning while Uncle Bob and I were recalling how much she adored carrots (she used to steal them out of George's shirt pocket), Uncle Ivan held up his hand, his eyes filled with pain.

"I can't," he whispered. "I just can't seem to talk about her." He hung his head.

"But why?" Uncle Bob asked. "I don't get it, big guy."

Uncle Ivan spread his arms wide. "It's this," he said. "We have all *this*. Space and food and sun and flowers and friends. It's just not fair. Stella should have had it, too."

After that, we stopped talking about Aunt Stella.

But we didn't stop remembering her. At least I didn't.

"I'm sorry," I say. "I didn't mean to make you sad."

The three of us look off into the distance, as if we're expecting Aunt Stella to join us.

"Don't sweat it, kid," Uncle Bob says. "Stella was a great gal. It's good to talk about folks you miss." He sends Ivan a *you should listen to me* look.

"That's oddly . . . mature advice," says Aunt Kinyani. She narrows her eyes. "What have you done with the real Bob?"

"I get zero respect around here," Uncle Bob mutters.

Everyone laughs and the dark mood lightens a little. But I can see in Uncle Ivan's faraway gaze that he hurts every bit as much as I do.

night

Before bedtime the keepers call us, and we all enter the Elephant Pavilion, a huge, high-ceilinged building. It's brand-new, built after a recent tornado destroyed many areas of the park, and it's full of hay and water, toys and treats, and lots of soft places to rest. (Elephants sleep in different ways and places, depending on how safe we feel. Here at the park, some of us lie down. But in the wild, elephants mostly doze upright.)

As nice as the pavilion is, though, I'd still rather be outside.

Aunt Laheli stops by to say good night. I'm in a quiet corner, toying with a green ball. "I just wanted to say night, and to tell you not to worry about your Tuskday, Ru-Ru," she says. She twirls a piece of hay with her trunk, then eats it.

A thought occurs to me. "If I didn't have tusks, would

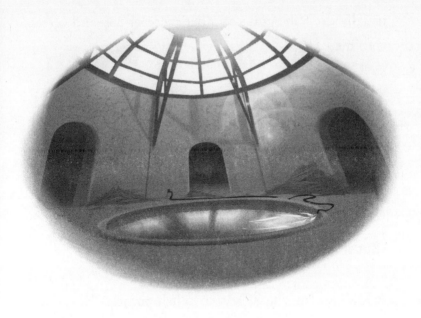

I still have to do my Tuskday?" I ask.

"Yeth," Aunt Laheli says, her mouth full. "Doesn't matter. Truth is, some elephants never grow tusks. They say that's happening more these days."

"I wonder why."

"Dunno. But I wouldn't be surprised if humans have something to do with it," says Aunt Laheli. "They usually do." She grabs another piece of hay and offers it to me.

"No thanks," I say. "I'm not really hungry."

"Suit yourself." Aunt Laheli chews noisily. "Here's the deal, Ruby. Tuskday is just our way of saying, 'Hey, look, you're growing up.'"

"But that's why we have birthdays," I point out.

"How can I put this?" Aunt Laheli pauses. "Birthdays are about *you*. Tuskdays are about *us*."

I plop down on my rear. Suddenly I'm tired. "Us who?"

"Us . . . us. Elephants. Tuskdays celebrate the herd. The earth. Everybody."

"That's not really very helpful, Aunt Laheli." I groan. "What if Aunt Akello asks me something I can't answer? What if I say the wrong thing? What if I fail the test?"

Aunt Laheli drapes her trunk around my neck. "It's not like that. I promise."

"Give me a hint, at least. What do I need to know?"

Aunt Laheli smiles at me with her good eye. "Whatever it is, it's already in your heart."

"If you really loved me, you'd tell me," I say. I figure it's worth a try.

"I really *do* love you. Which is why I'm not going to tell you." Aunt Laheli heads off. "Get some sleep, sweet Tusky," she calls. "Whoops! I mean—"

"That's all right, Aunt Laheli," I say, and I force a smile to show her I'm not mad.

I glance at the skylights overhead. Every now and then I catch a glimmer of the moon behind racing clouds.

I wonder if I will ever see moonlight without thinking of Aunt Stella.

mwezi

Aunt Stella loved the moon.

The cage she and I shared at the mall smelled like stale popcorn and moldy hay and animals who'd forgotten how to hope. But there was a skylight, and when the moon poured creamy light through the cracked glass, Aunt Stella would stare in wonder.

"Good evening, Mwezi," she would say. That's what she called the moon.

When it was cloudy and Mwezi disappeared, we couldn't sleep. Our cage felt spooky, like someone had turned off the lights and stolen our favorite white blanket.

Still, it wasn't all bad. It gave us an excuse to keep talking, and elephants in the wild don't sleep much, anyway. Just a couple of hours each day.

Sometimes Aunt Stella and I would talk all night long.
We always whispered so we wouldn't wake up Ivan and
Bob. But Ivan snored so loudly that we probably didn't
need to worry.

Every night I had a zillion questions.

I wanted to know why Uncle Ivan's tummy was so big.

I wanted to know why humans hid their tails.

I wanted to know if Uncle Bob could marry a cat.

But one question had no answer. I wanted to know why Aunt Stella and I had ended up at the Exit 8 Big Top Mall and Video Arcade. Why were we there, and not in Africa?

Aunt Stella didn't have an answer for that question.

Still, if we talked about it enough, she said, maybe we wouldn't dream about it.

Before I fell asleep each night, Aunt Stella always had two questions for me.

"So," she would say, "what amazed you today, sweet girl?"

Sometimes I would pretend to be asleep, because I couldn't think of an answer. But Aunt Stella wouldn't give up. She would stroke my back with her trunk, or nudge me softly with her head, and try again.

"C'mon, my Ruby," she'd say.

"What do you mean?" I'd ask every now and then, just to buy some extra time.

"I mean," said Aunt Stella, "what surprised you today? What filled you with wonder? What made you feel awe? That's what I mean by 'amazed.' Anything can be amazing, Ruby. Anything and everything."

She would look at me with such hope in those wise, weary eyes. Somehow I knew my answer—no matter what it was—would bring her a moment of joy.

I would think hard. I'd recall my day, second by second, minute by minute, because elephants are good at that. I wanted something that would make her smile.

Sometimes it took me a while to find an answer. It's hard to be amazed when you are living in a dirty cage.

But I always came up with something.

I would look out the dusty windows and say, "Fireflies amaze me, Aunt Stella. I wish I could make my rear end light up!"

Or I would watch Julia's dad clean the floors with his sudsy mop, and I would say, "Bubbles are amazing!

They're like tiny rainbows that pop."

Once after lunch, when Uncle Ivan treated us to the most awesome burp in the history of burps, I said, "Okay, I already know my amazing thing for today. Gorilla burps for sure, no contest."

After I answered, no matter what I said, Aunt Stella would gaze out at the moon and sigh the happy sigh I'd been hoping for.

But there was still one more question to come: "What made you proud today, little Ruby?"

"Well," I might answer, "I said 'thank you' when Uncle Ivan drew me a picture of a mouse. Also I didn't tell him it looked like an apple with whiskers, even though it kind of really did."

"Excellent," Aunt Stella would say, or "That's my gal!"

Once I'd answered, she would whisper, "I love you, Ruby," and I'd whisper back, "I love you even more, Aunt Stella," and only then could she fall asleep.

I'd listen as her steady breathing made gentle night music, and let myself find rest.

an elephant alone

Tonight I wonder if I'll ever fall asleep. I doubt it. Not with the moon playing hide-and-seek with the clouds. Not with questions buzzing in my brain like flies in a bottle.

I wander through the pavilion. Aunt Akello says the keepers make us go inside at bedtime for our own safety. And there are lots of things to do—enrichment, I think they call it. Food puzzles. Browse (branches covered in tasty leaves) hanging from ropes. Also, my favorite: pretend termite mounds with hidden treats.

But it's nothing like my life in the wild when I was a baby.

Back in Africa, we were always on the move. A herd can travel fifty miles a day or more, searching for water and food. We walked together, one by one, kind of like we were connected by an invisible thread. Even if you're just a tiny baby, you feel safe.

"I used to love night walking," Aunt Stella told me one time. "Nobody talking, just the sound of our feet moving and moving and moving like a heartbeat. It was like we'd become one giant animal. The herd heart, my grandmother used to call it."

Her voice had a lonely sound to it, so I patted her with my little trunk. "Don't be sad, Aunt Stella," I said. "I'm your herd now."

"You are my herd, dear one," she said. "And my heart."

The clouds parted for a moment, and Mwezi's light blanketed our cage. "It's just . . ." Aunt Stella shook her head. "It's just . . . wouldn't it be nice to be back with a herd? All of us moving together in the moonlight? Just imagine, Ruby."

"We'll have a herd again someday, Aunt Stella," I said, even though, of course, I had no idea if that was true.

"Perhaps," she said, just as Mwezi vanished again.

We stared into the darkness, and after a while I heard Aunt Stella whisper something: *An elephant alone is not an elephant.*

It was the Creed of the Herd. The very phrase Aunt Akello would someday ask me to memorize.

But the words didn't make any sense. I'd been alone, more times than I wanted to remember, and it wasn't like I'd ever stopped being me.

I mean, an elephant is an elephant is an elephant, right?

After a long while, I finally manage to doze off. I dream, as I sometimes do, of the bones.

I'm all alone on the savanna and they're gleaming in the moonlight, smooth and white and weirdly beautiful.

Every time I touch one, it turns to dust.

grumpy

In the morning, I feel tired and grumpy. Which is kind of not-me, because I love morning.

Morning means a scrumptious breakfast and pondplay and mudfun and who knows what else. Morning is like a gift you get to open every single day.

My aunt Zaina does not agree with me. She says mornings are an abomination, which I am pretty sure is not a good thing. She says she gets to be cranky until noon because she is the second oldest after Aunt Akello and she has earned the privilege to be unpleasant.

Today I decide she has the right idea, so I join Aunt Zaina by her favorite rock. She calls it her "shoulder boulder" because it's perfect for leaning. Sometimes she rests there all day, because she has arthritis in her feet after spending years penned up in a little cage in a crummy zoo.

Aunt Akello says Aunt Zaina needs to move her old bones more and she'll feel better. Aunt Zaina says her old bones beg to differ.

Aunt Zaina and I stand side by side. Neither of us says good morning.

"What's up?" she asks after a long while. She has an excellent, growly voice. "You're usually so peskily perky in the morning."

"I'm trying something new. I call it 'the grumpies.'"

"I approve," she says. "It's quite refreshing."

Aunt Elodie and Aunt Masika trot past. They are the same size and almost the same age, although they aren't related. Because they have similar extra-large ears and extra-long trunks, visitors often think they're twins.

Both Aunt Elodie and Aunt Masika love to sing. They sing *good morning* and *good night* and *how was your lunch* and *time for a dust bath.* They sing about anything and everything.

I think it's kind of sweet, even if they aren't always in tune. But Aunt Zaina says they would sing *Come and see our delightful dung!* if anyone would listen.

"Tomorrow's your Tuskday!" Aunt Elodie trills, and Aunt Masika echoes her: "Your Tuskday! Your Tuskday!"

I pretend to smile, but I doubt it's very convincing. I am a lousy actor.

We stare at an area near the border of Elephant Odyssey. The wire fence is covered with black material and yellow tape. "Wonder what they're up to over there?" Aunt Zaina says.

"Maybe they're making a bigger space for us," I say.

"You are an incurable optimist," says Aunt Zaina. "They're no doubt building something for themselves.

A store that sell T-shirts with our pictures on them, perhaps. Humans love making unnecessary things. Then they love buying the unnecessary things. Then they love throwing away unnecessary things."

"Maybe," I say, but I'm distracted by something interesting: a hole. A smallish, hard-to-see hole near a corner of the fence.

"So tomorrow's your Tuskday, eh?" Aunt Zaina asks. She doesn't sound particularly excited, but then, she never does.

"Yep," I say.

"Yep," she repeats.

"I guess I can't avoid it," I say.

"Nope," she says.

"Nope," I repeat.

"You can't run away from growing up," she says. "That's a race you will not win, my friend."

"Nope," I say.

"Nope," she agrees.

Aunt Zaina leans on her boulder, closes her eyes, and dozes off. She does that sometimes.

Quietly, I head off toward the hole in the fence. Because despite what Aunt Zaina says, maybe I can win the race, after all.

Or at least postpone it.

the hole

It's not a big hole, but it might be big enough. Especially if an elephant pushed on it. Hard.

If I ran away, maybe I wouldn't have to do my Tuskday.

A voice in my head says, *Ruby, don't be silly. You can't run away. There's nowhere to go.*

It says, *Even if you can sneak away for a while, they'll find you. You know very well that elephants aren't very easy to hide.*

It says, *This is really not a good plan, Ruby. You can delay your Tuskday. But not forever.*

Before I can argue back, I hear Aunt Akello calling me. I'll have to finish this conversation with myself another time.

"Ruby!" Aunt Akello calls. "Over here, dear!"

"Coming," I reply, trunk-trudging along.

Trunk-trudging is sort of the opposite of floppy-running. It's when you plod extra slow, dragging your trunk. Trunk-trudging is useful when you have to do annoying things, like go to bed or visit the vet or practice for your Tuskday.

As I near her, Aunt Akello points with her trunk. "It appears someone's looking for you. Over by the visitors' area."

That's not unusual. Lots of humans come to the park to see me. I'm not bragging. It's just a fact. When you're the littlest elephant, you end up with tons of fans.

I figure it's probably Carmen, a girl who visits me nearly

every week with her family. Carmen always starts to cry when her mother tells her it's time to leave the park. She says she wants to take me home with her. She wants me to be her pet and sleep in her bed and go to school with her for Sharing Time.

I don't think I would like being a pet elephant, although Uncle Bob is a pet (even though he claims he's not). He lives with people who take him on walks and feed him treats and rub his tummy. That sure sounds like a pet to me.

But Uncle Bob says he is a service dog, because he is providing the service of being charming.

When I get to the stone wall where most of the visitors are gathered, I look for Carmen, but she's nowhere to be found. Some of the people go, "Awwww!" when they see me. Lots of them take pictures.

I raise my trunk and give them my best Cute Baby Elephant pose, and that's when I hear it. A man's voice calling my name.

Not "Ruby."

One of my *old* names.

One of my Africa names.

jabori

I spread my ears wide and listen.

"Duni! Over here! Duni!"

It's Jabori's voice. Jabori's laugh. A big, loud, straight-from-the-belly laugh.

Jabori. My old friend from Africa. Jabori, alive and well.

At last I see him. Tall and slender and smiling ear to ear. Waving and jumping to be sure I see him. He's holding a map of the park and wearing a baseball cap, like lots of the visitors.

But Jabori isn't just any visitor.

Jabori saved my life. He cared for me when I was just a tiny, orphaned baby. He named me Duni, too.

My mother had called me "Nya," but Jabori didn't know that, of course.

Both of those names got left behind in Africa, like so many things.

I trumpet like crazy and dance around and do everything I can to say hello.

For a long time, kind of like forever, Jabori and I gaze at each other. I want so much to be close to him. To drape my trunk around his neck. To feel his hands patting my back. To hear him humming his silly elephant lullabies.

But my world is full of fences and walls now.

After a while, Jabori starts chatting with one of the park workers. Her name is Mandy, and she answers questions from visitors and gives talks about me and my aunts. Jabori points at me, Mandy nods, and they walk off together, threading their way through the crowd. Before he turns a corner, Jabori spins around and waves to me. This time, instead of "Duni," he calls, "Ruby!"

He spends a little extra time on the first part of my name: "Roooo-bee! Roooo-bee!" Like he's cheering me on. My biggest fan of all time.

After a moment, Jabori disappears into the crowd. I wait and wait, but he never returns.

I'm just about to head over to Canine Corner when Dawon, one of the elephant keepers, approaches me. He's carrying a big, juicy-looking apple, which he knows I love, and of course when he signals me to follow him, I do.

We're trained to obey the keepers' commands so they can take care of us. But I'll do anything for a free apple.

Dawon leads me toward a private walled-off area where we sometimes get checkups with T.J. or one of the other vets. For some reason, Mandy, the tour guide, is waiting there for us.

I feel a little suspicious, but when Dawon hands me the apple, I get distracted. Snacks will do that. I'm chomping away on the apple when, just on the other side of the brick wall, I see a baseball cap. "Roooo-bee!" a voice calls. "Duni!"

That's why Mandy and Dawon have brought me here!

This time there's no moat, and Jabori's so close I can reach over the wall, grab that silly hat of his, and toss it in the air, just like the old days.

So of course I do.

When Mandy unlocks a gate and Jabori enters, we run to each other and he hugs me like I'm the little orphan baby he cradled for so many nights, and even though I'm practically grown up and have tusks and everything, I let him.

It's the least I can do.

After Jabori and I say our goodbyes, I floppy-run to Canine Corner to see Uncle Ivan. Uncle Bob has just arrived with Julia.

Julia waves to me and I trumpet a hello.

"No funny business, you," she tells Uncle Bob.

He winks at me like always. "I can't help being funny."

"Back in half an hour," Julia calls as she heads off.

"Guess who I just saw?" I say to Uncle Ivan and Uncle Bob.

Uncle Bob scratches an ear. "Is this a riddle?"

"No, it's a for-real thing!" I exclaim. "I just saw my friend Jabori! He took care of me in Africa. At the elephant orphanage."

"Elephant what?" asks Uncle Ivan, tilting his big ol' head.

"It's where baby elephants went. If they didn't have a mom. Or an aunt. Or a herd. The ones who needed someone to take care of them."

Ivan plucks a piece of grass and gazes at it. I can tell he's wondering about something because his eyes have a special thinking look, soft and glowy like dawn clouds. "You never told us about that, Ruby."

"I didn't?" I ask. But as soon as the words are out of my mouth, I realize he's right. "I guess some things kind of don't want to get talked about," I say, even though it isn't much of an explanation. "You know how that is."

I'm thinking about Uncle Ivan and Aunt Stella, of course, but I don't say that part.

"So how did this Jabori fellow find you here?" asks Uncle Bob.

"I heard him tell Dawon and Mandy that he searched sanctuaries and zoos on his computer," I say. "He's here visiting family in the US."

"Humans love those laptop thingies," says Bob. "But if you can't chew it or chase it, I don't see the point."

I give the pond a little splash with my trunk. "It was so good to see Jabori and he hugged me lots and I even got to steal his hat like in the old days."

Ivan looks confused. That happens sometimes, even though he is a very wise gorilla. "You *stole* his hat?" he asks.

"It was our way of saying hello," I explain. "I would wrap my trunk around his shoulder, and then, when he didn't suspect anything, I would grab his hat with my trunk and make it fly through the air like a weird bird."

"And he liked this routine?" Uncle Bob asks.

"It made him laugh. Jabori laughs a lot!" I pause. "When I heard it today, I all of a sudden realized how much I missed it, and him. It made me so happy, and then I . . ."

Out of nowhere, I feel this frozen place inside me start to melt a little. I guess it was always there, but somehow I didn't realize it.

And now I'm crying and I don't even really know why.

help

Uncle Bob is pacing back and forth, and Uncle Ivan and Aunt Kinyani look like they're going to leap over the wall separating us.

"Ruby!" Uncle Ivan calls. "Please don't cry! Please! What's wrong?"

I swallow a sob. "I . . . I don't know. Seeing Jabori made me happy. But it also made me sad, 'cause I started remembering things."

"Take a deep breath and think about pineapples," Aunt Kinyani advises. "That always helps me."

I do as she says. But I do not really like pineapples, so I am still sad.

"Why don't you tell us more about your time in Africa?" Uncle Bob suggests. "Maybe that would make you feel better."

"More good advice from Bob." Aunt Kinyani shakes her head. "I am positively flummoxed."

"I'll take that as a compliment," says Bob.

"Go ahead, Ruby," says Uncle Ivan. He sends me an encouraging smile. "Tell us more about Jabori and the orphanage."

I take another deep breath. I think of pineapples one more time, but that still doesn't help.

So I begin.

my first day

"Do you remember what it was like when you were just born?" I ask.

Uncle Bob and Aunt Kinyani shake their heads. "To tell the truth, I have trouble remembering yesterday," Uncle Ivan says. "Although I *think* I had seven bananas for breakfast."

"It was nine, dear," says Kinyani.

"Well, I remember everything," I say. I sniffle, but talking is making me feel a little better already. "I remember lying on the hard ground and blinking at the brightness, even though I was hidden under my mama and it was the middle of the night."

"Whoa," says Uncle Bob. "Elephants really *do* have great memories."

"Everyone in my herd was there," I add. "I remember a forest of gray legs surrounding me, and all the trunks nuzzling me to say, 'Welcome, little one.' I even remember my big brother, Reth, running in circles, asking if I wanted to play chase.

"It took a little bit of time to figure out that I had four legs. Mama trunk-boosted me, helping me while I tried to get my balance. My legs wobbled, but I was standing."

"Amazing," says Uncle Ivan. "It takes human babies around a year to learn to walk."

Uncle Bob scratches an ear. "Well," he says, "those kiddos are a few fries short of a Happy Meal, if you catch my drift. Can't walk on their own, can't talk, don't even know how to poop outside."

It feels good to smile. "Yeah, elephant babies rule," I say. "I wish you could have been there. Everybody in the herd was so happy to see me. When Mama announced that my name would be Nya, there was

71

lots of rumbling and trumpeting and ear-flapping."
The memory makes me sigh. "I figured I must be
pretty special."

Uncle Ivan nods. "You were right about that, my girl."

messy

"Before long, I smelled something important and sweet. I didn't know what it was. But I knew that I needed it more than anything else in the world.

"I sniffed with my trunk, which was not helpful, because at first when you're a baby elephant your trunk doesn't always listen to you. You tell it to go up and it goes down. You tell it to go right and it goes left.

"Worse yet, *everything* tickles and makes you sneeze. The first time I sneezed, I fell over, it was such a surprise.

"Mama knew what to do, fortunately. She shifted a bit, just a step or two, and there it was: my first meal!

"I heard my brother laugh. Later he told me I was as messy as a warthog when I ate.

"But I was happy, and I was special, and I was surrounded by love. I had a feeling I was going to like being an elephant."

"How many elephants were in your herd, Ruby?" Uncle Ivan asks. "In my troop—that's a gorilla family—we had ten gorillas."

I stop to count. "Sixteen. A herd is a big ol' family. Mostly it's females. Sisters and aunts and moms and grandmothers. But there can be boys, too. When they get old enough, they head off with other guy elephants."

"That's a whole lot of elephants," says Uncle Bob.

"Yep," I say. "As soon as I was strong enough, we all started moving. The reason baby elephants learn to walk so quickly is 'cause they have to. Elephants are always traveling from one place to another in search of food and water, and fifty miles a day is a lot of walking."

"No way could I knuckle walk that far," says Uncle Ivan.

"Me neither," says Uncle Bob. "I am cursed with the burden of teeny, tiny, adorable legs."

"You would have loved where I lived," I say. "The savanna is huge and beautiful and sometimes scary. (Like Aunt Akello.) It's grassland mostly, with dry and rainy seasons, although there wasn't nearly enough rain when I was there. Sometimes it's green and growing, and sometimes the land looks sort of sick and thirsty. During a drought, the grass turns brown and bristly, and dust sticks to you like you're wearing a coat.

"Everybody's kind of connected on the savanna. Mama taught me that right away. Dung beetles and cheetahs, vultures and giraffes, rock pythons and hyenas. Everybody.

"'Course, it's not like we were all best buddies. There aren't any fences or walls on the savanna, which means you always have to be on the lookout for somebody who wants to eat you. Lucky for me, elephants are so powerful that we don't really have to be as afraid as smaller animals."

"Same with gorillas," says Uncle Ivan. "We just had to worry about humans."

"On the other hand, *everybody* wants to eat a guy who's my size," Uncle Bob grumbles.

"Well, hyenas and lions and other animals with sharp teeth will eat elephant babies if they get the chance," I say. "That's why calves are always protected by their herd."

In Africa, I think to myself, *an elephant alone is not an elephant for long.*

gichinga

"Every day on the savanna was kind of the same: walking, eating, drinking, playing, resting.

"But mostly walking.

"Sometimes I would grab Mama's tail when we walked. She didn't mind. She was a great mom, always checking on me, being an elebrella, feeding me whenever I wanted.

"And it was awesome, having so many relatives on hand to provide advice and a helping trunk.

"Mama was called Bishara, and she was so pretty! She had long legs and beautiful tusks. When she trumpeted, she could make the whole savanna tremble. (Even me.) I was her second calf. Her first, my brother, Reth, was four years older than me.

"Reth was fun, but he was awfully noisy and rambunctious. Mostly I played with my friend Gichinga, who happened to be a cattle egret.

"Cattle egrets are these small whitish birds with long beaks. They're nice, but some of them can be a little pushy. Whenever you see a herd of elephants, you'll probably see a flock of cattle egrets riding on top of them, acting like they're in charge of the whole wide world.

"When elephants walk, our heavy feet kick up all kinds of things, especially dirt and brush and grasses, where lots of insects live. Since cattle egrets love to eat bugs, when they stay near elephants, it's like they're at an all-day restaurant and we're the cooks.

"In return, the cattle egrets squawk like crazy when they know a bad guy like a lion is coming. That gives the grown-up elephants time to gather their calves close so they can be extra protected.

"Gichinga hopped on my back when I was three days

old. He was just a little guy himself, the smallest of his brood. Maybe that's why he decided to hang out with me.

"In any case, even my little feet kicked up a fair number of bugs, and I was almost always right next to Mama, so Gichinga got twice the food in return for sitting on me all day."

"The first time Gichinga landed on my back, I turned my head and said, 'Hey, who invited you?'

"'Oh, pardon me!' he exclaimed in a squeaky voice. 'Is this seat taken?'

"'As a matter of fact,' I said, 'it's *my* seat.'

"'I thought . . . I mean, I was told that this is how it's done,' Gichinga said. 'If you look about, you'll see what I mean.'

I glanced around. Sure enough, a bunch of white birds sat on the backs of my relatives. Grandmama, our matriarch, even had two cattle egrets on her. I watched as one flitted off her back to snatch a big ol' bug, then came back to enjoy his meal.

"'If you let me stay, I can eat bugs that annoy you,'

Gichinga said. He flapped his wings. 'And if there are any hyenas coming, I'll warn you.'

"'That's why we have Grandmama and the others,' I said.

"'Well, she doesn't eat mosquitoes, does she?' Gichinga asked.

"'Not on purpose.'

"'There you have it, then,' he said. 'My name is Gichinga, by the way. What's yours?'

"'They call me Nya,' I said.

"Gichinga hopped a little closer to my head. 'Can you whistle?'

"'Nope,' I said, 'but I'm learning to trumpet.'

"Before long, we became our own little band. I would thump my feet, and Gichinga would start a trill, and then I would add a huff or a puny trumpet, and back and forth we would go until one of the aunts would tell us to cut it out."

possible

"Gichinga was my very first friend.

"A first friend is a true gift, because forever after, your heart knows what's possible."

I glance over at my friends. "I'm sorry," I say. "Am I talking too much?"

"No!" Uncle Ivan exclaims. "Please tell us more, Ruby."

"I was wondering," says Uncle Bob, "when you first ran into humans. That must have been a shock."

"Actually," I say, "long before I ever saw any humans, I smelled them."

"Yep." Uncle Bob nods. "They do have a distinctive . . . odor."

"Gichinga and I noticed the smell at the same time.

"When I asked Mama what the weird, sour smell

drifting on the wind was, she said, 'That's the smell of danger, Nya. Remember it.'

"And I did, too. Not that it would matter."

"A few days later, I learned about another scent to watch out for: smoke.

"It was just a little hint on the breeze. But as soon as I caught my first whiff, I knew it was bad. I knew to be afraid.

"How could that be, even? How could I have known about something I'd never even run into before?

"Grandmama said it was elephant wisdom, passed down through the generations. She told me that when she was my age, fires hardly ever happened. Now, she said, with the world so dry and the sun so hot, she was certain this wouldn't be the last smoke I smelled.

"'Should we run?' I asked her, and she shook her head. 'No, Nya. That smoke is far, far away. It's not a danger to us.'

"'But how will I know if it is?' I asked, tugging on her tail.

"'You'll know,' was all she said."

thirst

"After a few weeks, I noticed a worried feeling hanging over the herd like a swarm of gnats. I didn't understand what it all meant. But I knew that everyone was hungry and thirsty. Even Mama's milk wasn't always there for me, no matter how much she wanted it to be.

"Another drought had hit the land, Mama said. Grandmama's long-used trails, the ones that linked water hole to water hole, couldn't be counted on.

"From the other elephants, I learned that there are different kinds of thirst.

"There's 'I've been playing hard and I could use a slurp of water.'

"There's 'I really, really need to drink something. Now.'

"There's 'I feel weak, I'm scared, please, please find me something, anything. Even a drop will do.'

"That last one is the kind of thirst that comes when the rains do not."

bad places

"Twice, searching for water and food, Grandmama led us into places we were not supposed to go.

"We only realized they were bad places when the humans began to yell.

"It's hard for us to tell where farms begin and wild lands end. A herd can do a whole lot of damage if it wanders through farmland and eats crops. But it's not our fault. It's just the way we are. We have big tummies and we need to fill them.

"The humans made hard, hurting noises that ripped the air, and we stampeded to safety.

"Hunting rifles, Mama explained later, as I trembled under her belly."

the mud hole

"The next time I met up with humans, we were even closer to some farms.

"Mama and I had been straggling behind the herd more and more. We were both weak, and keeping up is already tough when you're just a tiny calf. The herd tried to wait patiently, and Grandmama did her best to slow the pace. But she was responsible for everyone, not just us.

"Even Gichinga switched to the back of a faster elephant, one of my younger aunts, when his mother insisted he leave me behind.

"'I understand,' I told him. 'Don't worry. We'll catch up before you know it.'

"But I missed our little band, and it was hard not to feel hurt, even though I knew he was just obeying his mother, who was trying to keep him safe and well fed.

"Somehow, later that morning, the herd moved far enough ahead of us that we lost sight of them completely.

"'We'll be fine, little one,' Mama said, but I could hear something new and nervous in her voice.

"We followed the herd's trail as well as we could, but when we caught the surprising scent of mud and water, Mama hesitated. Even though the smell of humans was strong, she just couldn't pass up the possibility of finding water.

"Sure enough, we came upon a small mud hole, not much bigger than me, but beautiful to our eyes.

"I ran toward it so fast that I slid down the steep bank straight to the muddy bottom.

"The water wasn't very deep, and at least it was wet. But the mud was thick, and it sucked me down until I was belly-deep.

"I screamed. I was so, so scared! Mama tried hard to reach me with her trunk, but I was just too far away.

"When we heard the humans running toward us, we knew the end was near."

good humans

"The humans gathered around the hole. There were many of them, and they made sounds with their mouths.

"I'd never heard humans speak before. The noises they made were strange. Nicer than hyena squeals. But not nearly as lovely as birdsong.

"Mama paced back and forth, back and forth, while the humans lowered thick ropes and tied them around my tummy. I should have been terrified. I hadn't forgotten what Grandmama had said about humans and danger.

"But something told me I was going to be all right. 'Don't worry, Mama,' I called. 'They're helping me.'

"I was right. After an hour of pushing and pulling and grunting and struggling, the humans yanked me out of that hole.

"I was safe! Scared and shivering, but safe.

"They even led us back toward our herd.

"I'll never forget their kindness, even in a zillion years. Those were good humans. My first, but not my last."

"Good humans." Uncle Ivan repeated the words slowly, like he was tasting them for the first time. "I've met a few of them myself."

Uncle Bob groaned, but after a moment, he shrugged. "Okay. I hate to admit it, Ivan, but you're right. Take Julia and her mom and dad. They're not too shabby, as humans go."

"On the other hand," I said, and Uncle Ivan and Aunt Kinyani and Uncle Bob all sat up straight, afraid of what was coming next.

"On the other hand?" Uncle Bob asked.

"On the other hand," I said softly, "there were the bones."

the bones

"We came across the bones under a small acacia tree.

"It was a few days after Mama and I had caught up to the herd at last. We were still stragglers at the end of the line. But at least we were back where we belonged.

"The bones lay in a pile, with a few scattered here and there, but I didn't know what they were. Even after Reth whispered, 'Uh-oh. I don't like the look of those.' Even after the whole herd gathered quietly around the pile.

"'What are they, Mama?' I asked.

"'Those are elephant bones, Nya. When we see those, we stop whatever we are doing,' she said. 'We see a life that has happened and we honor it. We feel the wind and the sun on our backs, and we are glad and grateful to be alive.'

"In a way, they were beautiful, the bones. Glowing in the harsh sun. Curling and twisting. Some thick as a small tree trunk. Some thin as a twig.

"Grandmama went first, while the rest of us watched. It was eerily quiet. As if the whole savanna was holding its breath.

"I'd seen Grandmama pick a single blade of grass with her heavy trunk. I'd seen her pluck a bug off a leaf, unhurt, and let him fly off into the clouds. But the way she touched those bones was gentler still.

"The first bone was long and smooth. She ran the tip of her trunk the length of it. Learning the scent. Knowing it.

"Some of the older aunts followed Grandmama's lead. They moved close to the pile, breathing, touching, considering. Nobody spoke.

"When Mama reached out her trunk to touch the

bones, I rushed to join her. I almost stepped on a thin bone, and one of the aunts yanked me back with her trunk. 'Foolish calf!' she snapped, and behind me I heard Reth snicker.

"I chose to ignore him.

"'Gently,' Mama said as I extended my trunk. I could just barely reach a small, curved bone. It lay on the dirt like a tiny new moon that had lost its way.

"I inhaled, careful not to breathe too hard, because what if I sneezed after already almost squishing a bone?

"I felt other pieces. I saw how they could weave together to be something more. Something that could move and grow and cup a beating heart.

"'Mama?' I said.

"'Yes, Nya?'

"'Where are her tusks?'

"Mama and Grandmama looked at each other. 'We may never know,' Mama answered at last.

"'I don't understand,' I said.

"Soon enough I would."

after

"Two days later, we fell behind again, Mama and me.

"That's when it happened.

"One shot. Like a crack of thunder. A rock split in two.

"Like a heart breaking.

"After Mama died, I lay by her side in the blistering sun.

"I would stay, I decided, until our bones turned white together."

"As I lay there, out of nowhere, two young bull elephants darted from a clump of trees, galloping toward me.

"'Up, little one,' the larger one urged, nudging me with his trunk. 'You've got to hurry. They're coming for the tusks.'

"The tusks.

"*Her* tusks.

"I didn't move.

"'Now!' the smaller one cried as another shot rang out.

"They both pushed me hard with their tusks. 'Now, if you want to live!' the smaller one yelled again, and I suppose some part of me did, because at last I stood and followed them to safety in the trees.

"We waited silently while the poachers did what they'd come to do. The bulls made sure I couldn't see what was happening.

"But I didn't need my eyes to know.

"For another day, those two bulls—I never did find out their names—tried to look out for me. But they were young, and they didn't know the first thing about caring for a baby. They had no milk to give me, of course. No way to really help.

"Still, they tried. They sheltered me from the worst of the heat. They told me wild stories about the trouble they'd gotten into. (There was a lot to tell.) They promised me I would be all right.

"How kind they were, those two! I was so sad. So scared. And they kept me from giving up completely.

"I just wish I'd had a chance to thank them."

"The next morning, it swooped from the sky.

"It wasn't a bird, I knew that much. A huge insect, maybe. One with big, stiff wings. It made a *thud-thud-thud* sound, like a slow stampede.

"The bulls looked at each other and I saw their terror.

"'Nya,' said the larger one, 'we have to run.'

"'But——' I began, just as the giant bug dropped close, churning up clouds of dust.

"The bulls were already running. One went right. One went left. I didn't know which to follow, and as the insect dipped even closer, I couldn't move. I felt like a tree, rooted to the ground.

"Fear can make you panic. But sometimes it floods

your body like cobra venom and leaves you frozen.

"I watched, helpless, as the insect settled on the ground."

the insect

"Just a few elephant-widths away, there it was, with wings like giant flat thorns. Its body was mango-shaped, and its tail didn't move. It hummed to itself, and the ground vibrated beneath my feet." I shivered at the memory. "And oh! It smelled so awful!"

"The insect had something inside it, moving quickly. Three humans leapt out of its stomach. They were heading toward me.

"I jerked my head left, right. I watched as one of the humans raised a stick. It was black and long, glinting in the sun.

"She pointed it directly at me."

pain

"A sharp noise came. Then an echo, and a burning feeling in my left flank.

"It wasn't too bad, really, so I tried to move, but with each step my feet grew heavier, heavier, until the ground seemed to call to me. 'Nya,' it sang, 'just rest for a moment.'

"'Just for a moment.'

"'Just for . . .'"

flying

"When I woke, my body felt heavy as a mountain. My legs were bound. I couldn't move. I could barely open my eyes.

"Somehow the humans had loaded me into the insect's belly. With the four of us squeezed inside, it headed toward the clouds. Was it really possible? Could I, a baby elephant, be flying through the air like a bird?

"I felt something on my side. It was one of the humans, patting me gently. I think he was saying things, too, but I couldn't hear over the throbbing noise of the insect.

"We landed a short time later with a big ol' thump. The insect fell silent and the humans jumped out.

"Through my half-opened eyes, I caught a glimpse of dirt and grass and more humans. But where was I?

"Was I anywhere near my herd? My old life?

"Could I find them again?

"Could I fight my way to freedom?

"I remembered the bulls I'd seen play-fighting. I was tiny compared to them, and I had no tusks.

"I tried to trumpet. I sounded like a sad little toad.

"I thought of Mama. What was the point in fighting, anyway?

"I closed my eyes and tried not to remember Mama's warm body, lying next to mine as the life slowly vanished from her."

"More humans appeared, and there was much talking and hand waving.

"Some joined me inside the insect. Others waited nearby.

"They pushed. They pulled. They made loud, angry noises, and sure enough, they began to move me out of the insect onto a new place: another, different creature.

"This one was grumbly and stinky. Its back was flat and it had four round feet.

"I didn't even try to fight. My legs were tied, my body was weak, and there was nowhere to go.

"And so I went on another strange ride in what turned out to be called a 'truck.' At least this one was on solid ground, something I understood.

"Four foul-smelling humans sat next to me. I could smell the savanna, too, dusty and familiar.

"I could not smell my herd.

"But I did smell elephants.

"The longer we moved, the more I began to sense other elephants nearby. Where, I couldn't be sure. But they were close.

"When we finally stopped, the place reeked of humans.

"But it also smelled like me. Like baby elephants.

"Lots and lots of them."

"Again there was much chattering from the humans. After a while, they pushed me down a small metal ramp to the ground. I was lying on my side.

"Carefully they cut the ties on my front and rear legs. They made calming noises as I tried to stand. I was still a little woozy, so two of the humans helped me stand. I wobbled like I had the day I was born. But I was upright, at least.

"I took one step, then another. Around me, the humans made soothing sounds and showed their teeth. (Later I would learn that's called 'smiling.')

"Later I would learn many important things.

"But where were the babies I'd smelled? And why were

their scents happy and calm, while I was trembling and terrified?

"When a bunch of the humans herded me into a large wooden cage, I didn't resist much. (Though I did attempt a couple of lame charges to scare them off. It didn't work. They just showed me their teeth and kept pushing.)

"The cage was made of pieces of wood, one stacked on another. It had a wide door, and the ceiling was high, higher even than Grandmama. Wood was everywhere! It was like being caught in a stand of trees without any leaves.

"There was hay underfoot, though, clean and sweet-smelling, and fresh water, at last.

"I looked up to see a tall, thin human standing in the doorway. He was wearing loose coverings over his skin, like the other humans, and a silly round thing on top of his head.

"He smiled, and then he made the most wonderful noise, like water bubbling up from deep underground.

"That was the first time I heard Jabori laugh."

introductions

Uncle Ivan smiled. "Ahh," he said. "Jabori! The friend you saw today."

I nodded. "Yep. Funny thing is, I should have been terrified. Grandmama's warning about humans was blaring in my head. But Jabori made it impossible to be afraid.

"I can't explain it.

"Maybe it was because he smelled like an elephant. The scent of other calves was on his clothes, his hands, his shoes.

"Maybe it was the way he constantly sang or hummed or talked in that soft, low, wind-in-the-trees voice.

"Maybe it was the way he knew what I needed before I knew what I needed.

"I've never met a human who understood elephants as well as Jabori, and I doubt I ever will."

"There's a word elephants have for those who take care of us. We call them 'sentinels.'

"A sentinel is someone who looks out for you. It can be someone who's part of your herd, of course, but it could be anyone. Sentinels can be your caretakers or your friends or your teachers or your neighbors.

"They look out for you. They understand you. They help you.

"Sentinels make you feel safe.

"Jabori was my sentinel.

"My mama was a sentinel, of course, and my grand-mama. My African herd was. Gichinga, too. The two bulls who'd saved my life. The humans flying in the giant insect, and the others who had helped (although it took me a while to realize that)."

I looked at Uncle Ivan and Uncle Bob. My eyes were hot with tears. "You," I said. "You are my sentinels."

I sniffled a little. "I'm a very lucky elephant."

what jabori knew

"Jabori knew I always needed a blanket draped over my back at night. The blankets were thick and heavy, and my favorite one had dots that reminded me of mud spatters, and long stripes that reminded me of elephant paths.

"Jabori knew I would be hungry, right on schedule, every three hours.

"Jabori knew just how to scratch an elephant ear.

"Jabori knew, when I dreamed of awful things and thrashed and moaned, that putting his arm around me and humming softly would help me find peace again.

"And Jabori knew that I needed a name. A new name, for my new life. He called me 'Duni,' and before long, 'Nya' was just a fading memory, like a morning star.

"I think maybe Jabori may have been part elephant."

"He started with food.

"Jabori understood what mattered to a baby elephant.

"Right away he brought me something in a dented bucket. I heard a sloshing sound, like water in a puddle. I sniffed the bucket with my trunk and took a step backward.

"Talking and humming as he worked, Jabori dipped his fingers into the bucket. He waved his hand near my trunk, then put his fingertips to my mouth.

"Again and again: fingers in bucket, fingers to trunk, fingers to mouth.

"Whatever it was, it was a little bit sweet and a little

bit salty, and it made my mouth water and my trunk twitch.

"It wasn't my mama's milk, but I wasn't in a position to be picky.

"In minutes, I was gulping from that bucket. What a mess I made!

"Reth would have laughed at me, but I didn't care. It had been a long time since my tummy had been so happy."

Bob smiles. "There is nothing," he says, "like a bite to eat when you're sure you'll never see food again."

an improvement

"After two days of the messy bucket, Jabori brought me something new.

"It was shaped like a small, clear log, and I could see liquid sloshing inside.

"Jabori held the log upside down and a couple drops plopped to the ground. I sniffed them and knew at once that it was the same almost-Mama's-milk I'd been drinking from the bucket.

"Gently Jabori held out the white log. I tested it with my trunk. It was smooth and cool.

"I touched the end. It was soft and movable, like hardening honey.

"I trusted Jabori. But this thing did not make any sense.

"Unless . . . I thought of my mother, and all at once I understood.

"The bottle was much easier for me to drink from, and far less messy. I felt Jabori's hand stroking my back as I ate hungrily.

"When I was done, I burped so loudly that Jabori laughed until his eyes watered."

the elephant orphanage

"Although I didn't know it then, the place where Jabori cared for me was called an 'elephant orphanage.'

"Jabori was one of many caretakers, all working together like bees in a hive.

"The orphanage was a special place for baby elephants who'd been found lost and alone. The way it worked was pretty simple. With pretend milk and pretend parents and a pretend life, they were trying to teach us how to survive.

"But the love was never pretend. Never."

"Mornings came really early at the orphanage, before the stars had run away. It was the stirring babies that woke me, with their shuffling and tiny trumpets. Each one was in a wooden enclosure like mine, and each one had a human companion, all day and all night.

"In my space there was an extra roommate. His name was Odongo, and he was a young African hedgehog. He was round and spiky, with bright, beady eyes and tiny feet.

"Odongo had been using my place as his home long before I'd gotten there. But he was happy enough to share the space with Jabori and me.

"He was a quiet roommate, but he liked to sit on my back the way Gichinga used to. And when I had bad dreams at night about Mama, he would cuddle up next to Jabori and me.

"Aside from Odongo, I hadn't yet met any of my other neighbors.

"As I calmed a bit, I grew more curious about the other elephants. Each day I heard a small group of babies head out into the open with their caretakers.

"Where did they go? If I went, too, would I find my family?

"The babies came back tired, smelling of dirt and sweet leaves.

"They seemed content, even happy.

"I wanted to know more."

"Soon enough, I had some answers, when I was allowed to join the other babies on their daily adventures.

"The first time Jabori led me out of my cage to the common area, the babies welcomed me with nuzzles and trumpets and nudges, as if we'd known each other forever.

"There were seventeen elephants at the orphanage while I was there. I was in an area called 'the nursery,' along with five other babies. We were separated from the older calves.

"I never learned how the other babies had ended up at the orphanage. I wasn't there long enough to ask, and nobody talked about their pasts.

"Sometimes, though, at night, I'd hear one of the babies cry out, and I'd know I wasn't the only one having bad dreams."

milk and mud

"Mornings at the orphanage were busy. Before leaving, we all chowed down on our breakfast milk. The huge bottles arrived in a wheelbarrow, and sometimes one of us would try to sneak an early drink.

"Once we were fed, it was time to begin our walk. Because of the drought, the only mud puddle we could visit was shallow, and just big enough for three babies at a time. But that didn't stop us from trying to squeeze the whole group in.

"Wallowing in mud was my favorite thing to do. Gooey and cool and messy, it was the best. We splashed and tumbled while our caretakers watched to be sure we didn't get carried away.

"Which of course we did. There is nothing better in the whole wide world than being totally covered in mud."

"After some mudfun, we'd turn to foraging. Even though we were still just drinking milk, it was good practice for when we got older.

"It was hard work, looking for leaves and grasses and grabbing them with our trunks. It seemed so easy when the grown-ups did it. But they had tusks, and they'd had lots of practice.

"One morning I stuck my trunk into a scrubby bush, hoping to discover a tender leaf or two, when a strange white-winged creature hit me in the forehead. It didn't hurt. I didn't actually feel anything, to tell the truth.

"But it scared me with its frantic fluttering.

"I reared back and tripped on my own feet, landing on another baby, who rolled into two others. They panicked and dashed off as fast as their little legs could manage, and suddenly we were all running, baby elephants and caretakers alike.

"It was only when Jabori produced a deafening whistle that we stopped short.

"Fanaka, the oldest baby, looked at me and said, 'You realize that was just a moth, right?'

"'A moth?' I repeated. 'But it was so big!'

"The other babies began to giggle.

"'You're an elephant, Duni,' Fanaka reminded me. 'You're, um, about a zillion times bigger than a moth.'

"'Well, it bonked me on the head! Hard!' I cried. 'And I'm telling you, it was gigantic!' But even I could hear how ridiculous I sounded.

"For a few days, the other babies called me 'Monster Moth,' but they got over it eventually.

"That was the first time I learned how useful it is to be able to laugh at yourself."

"By evening we were all exhausted, but before sleep, Jabori and I always had the same ritual. It involved the silly thing Jabori insisted on wearing on top of his head: a baseball cap.

"'Course, back then, I didn't know it was called a baseball cap. I just knew it was fun to steal.

"It worked like this. Jabori would bend down and lean close for a hug, and I would wrap my trunk around his shoulders. Then, just as he pulled away, I would snatch his cap and toss it in the air toward Odongo.

"It was a pretty good flyer. Like a round bird.

"Odongo would grab the cap when it landed (and sometimes even catch it), then run to a corner and bury it in the hay.

"I sure loved that game.

"Jabori pretended to be annoyed. But I think he loved it, too."

"One hazy, hot morning, I had to stay behind in my cage at the nursery while the others went out for their daily walk. I'd stepped on an acacia thorn the day before, and my right front foot was sore and swollen.

"Jabori fed me, tended to my foot, and kissed the top of my head. He said some words, then held up a finger, which I'd learned meant 'Wait here. I'll be back soon.'

"I watched him go and made a pouty face.

"'Some of the keepers are sick, I hear,' said Odongo, who was sniffing through the hay for any interesting food. 'Jabori has to help out.'

"'I'm stuck here all day,' I complained. 'But at least you and I can play.'

"'Sorry, no can do,' said Odongo. 'I've got to search for

breakfast. Some of us have to work for our food.'

"I watched him slip through a hole in the wood. 'See ya soon!' I called.

"I had no idea how wrong I was."

a hint of smoke

"The morning wore on. I tried to sleep, but I didn't want to. I built a little tower with pieces of hay, but it was boring. I listened for other elephants or keepers, but the place was strangely quiet.

"When I first noticed it, I thought I was imagining things. Maybe one of the keepers was cooking something. Maybe someone was smoking one of those awful-smelling cigarette thingies. (Although why a human would do *that* was beyond me.)

"But I wasn't imagining things.

"It was smoke. The kind of smoke that Grandmama had warned me about. The kind that meant danger.

"I trumpeted loudly to get someone's attention. Nothing.

"I called for Odongo to warn him. Nothing.

"I checked the sky, but there wasn't anything to see. Not yet, anyway.

"Why weren't the caretakers panicking? Didn't they smell what I smelled?

"But of course they didn't. Mama had told me once that humans can't detect scents nearly as well as elephants can. 'Just one of their many flaws,' she'd said.

"Jabori! Where was he? With the other babies on their walk? Had any of them sensed the danger yet?

"I pushed hard on the door to my cage. It didn't budge.

"I inhaled deeply. I wasn't wrong. There *was* smoke in the air, maybe even more of it.

"I ran hard against the door.

"One, two, three times. Nothing.

"I turned around and aimed for the back of the cage, where the wood was a bit splintered and warped.

"*Bam. Bam. Bam.*

"On my fourth try, I barreled through.

"I was outside. I was free. And I was alone.

"But now what?"

"The smell of smoke is a different kind of smell. It's alive. You can taste it in your trunk and your mouth and even deep inside you.

"You know it wants to hurt you.

"I was panicking and I knew it. But I couldn't stop myself.

"Maybe it was because I was so little. Maybe because I'd already been through so much. But with every breath, all I could hear was Grandmama in my head: *Danger. Danger. Danger.*

"I wanted to find Jabori. To warn Odongo. To herd the other elephants and caretakers to safety.

"But where were they? By this time of day, they'd be several miles out, foraging, and with my hurt foot, it would take forever to reach them.

"Maybe if I could find a caretaker close by and alert him, that would work. But the area was strangely deserted, probably because so many of them were sick today.

"I spun around, frantic to find someone, anyone. At the top of a small rise were a few cabins where some of the workers lived. It wasn't too far, and maybe from that height I could see Jabori and the others.

"I ran as fast as I could. Which was not very.

"The whole way there, all I could think was *danger, danger, danger,* like some horrible song that wouldn't end."

the cabin

"By the time I reached the top of the hill, my foot was throbbing and smoke was clearly visible, billowing in the air.

"I paused, trying to catch my breath, and looked around me. I could see the orphanage at the bottom of the hill. But I couldn't find Jabori and the other elephants and caretakers.

"Three cabins sat side by side. When I pushed with my trunk on the door of the first one, it swung open easily. I stepped inside, hoping to find one of the workers. But the place was silent.

"I'd never been in a human habitat before. It was impossibly big, compared to the place where Jabori and I slept each night, and filled with strange objects.

"Obstacles were everywhere, soft and oddly shaped,

like weird bushes. The floor had no hay at all. One room smelled of human food. In another room, blankets stretched across a flat expanse raised off the floor. I saw a pillow like the one Jabori liked to place his head on (when he wasn't using me for a pillow).

"The panic was tightening my chest. *Danger, danger, danger.*

"I delivered my loudest ever trumpet. Maybe someone would hear me. Maybe someone would wonder why a baby elephant was in a cabin built for humans.

"But nobody answered, and nobody came."

the fire

"I ran to the back room. *Jabori. Danger. Help.*

"I knew I wasn't thinking clearly. But the air was growing gray with smoke, and when I peered out the window, I could see flames heading up the hill.

"My eyes stung. Breathing hurt.

"I coughed so hard that I landed on the soft, flat surface with the blankets. A bed! My first and last, and even though the air was hot and bitter and I was pretty sure I was going to die, for a moment I thought, 'Wow. These humans sure do know how to sleep.'

"*Run. Danger. Run.*

"I got off the bed (not easy, when you're an elephant).

"I ran back outside.

"I couldn't see, couldn't breathe, couldn't think.

"So I just plain ran, blindly and without hope, down a trail on the far side of the hill.

"I didn't care where it led. As long as there wasn't a fire at the end of it."

at the bottom of the hill

"And then I saw them.

"Waiting at the bottom of the hill, as if they'd known I was coming.

"Four humans in a truck.

"Not workers from the orphanage.

"Not good humans.

"Four humans with dart guns. Four humans with ropes.

"For all I knew, they'd started the fire, and I was sure they would try to hurt me.

"But what choice did I have?"

"The four men were very happy to see me.

"I didn't have any tusks.

"But I was a baby elephant, and that was enough.

"People will pay good money for a baby elephant."

all of it

I stop for a moment and take a breath. Uncle Ivan and Aunt Kinyani and Uncle Bob are staring at me. I can see the worry in their eyes. I can almost feel the pain in their hearts.

"I'm . . . I'm sorry," I whisper.

"Don't be sorry," Uncle Ivan says. "Go on, Ruby. Just tell us the rest."

"Are you sure?" I ask.

"I'm sure," he says. "We need to hear it all."

travels

"There were many trucks after that.

"There was hiding.

"There was moving at midnight.

"There was thirst, and hunger.

"And sadness, blacker than a night without stars. What had happened to Jabori? To Odongo? To the other babies? Would I ever see them again?"

"When the land finally came to an end, the men took me to a long, floating thing called a 'ship.' It lay like a giant fish on top of salt-scented water called 'ocean.' The water went on forever and never stopped moving. Here and there, peaks of white foam popped up like busy little clouds.

"I lived in a dark, dung-filled crate. It rocked with the ocean until I was too sick to eat.

"Not that there was much to eat.

"After endless days, the ship found land. I was loaded into yet another truck for yet another long journey."

my new home

"My new home was a traveling road show called the Fizzle Brothers Family Circus.

"The Fizzle Brothers Family Circus wasn't really a circus. It was two trailers by the side of the road. A children's ride that squeaked and spun. It was small tents and sullen humans.

"They named me 'Ruby.' At first I hated the name. I was Nya. Or Duni. What did these awful humans know about me? What gave them the right to change my name?

"But after a while, I grew used to the sound of 'Ruby.' It was hard enough just remembering that I'd been a wild, free creature. I didn't have the energy to worry about what I'd been called.

"Most days, I walked in a circle behind another elephant, named Fiona. She'd probably had other names, too.

"Fiona wore an oily, worn saddle strapped to her back. People rode her for money. It cost extra to take a photo.

"Sometimes children kicked Fiona to see if she would go faster.

"She wouldn't.

"Fiona wasn't like Aunt Stella. She didn't talk to me much, didn't seem to care about anything. I could see from her empty eyes that she had given up a long time ago.

"Not that I could blame her."

"I wasn't with the Fizzle Brothers Family Circus for long. They lost all their money and sold me off to a guy named Mack.

"I guess you could say they fizzled.

"I was easy to sell because everyone loves elephant babies.

"Aunt Stella was in a traveling circus for a long, long time. I was only with the Fizzle Brothers for a month.

"I don't know how she did it."

how

I look at Uncle Ivan.

He looks back at me.

"I don't know, either," he says.

another home

"When I got to the Big Top Mall and Video Arcade at Exit 8, I still remember the moment before the doors opened.

"I was bruised and skinny and confused. I was too sick to be afraid.

"But I had been in trucks before. I knew that whatever was on the other side of those heavy metal doors, it wouldn't be good.

"The doors creaked. I blinked. The sun hurt my eyes after the dark inside of the truck.

"I saw two men. One was big and loud. The other had a gentle smile and a carrot in his shirt pocket. A little girl with long black hair stood nearby, her eyes wide. Beyond them was a huge darkish space with strange odors coming out of it.

"One really big smell was something I'd never run into before."

I smile at Uncle Ivan. "That turned out to be you," I say.

"He is remarkably fragrant," Uncle Bob says.

"Thank you, Bob," Uncle Ivan says. He winks at me. "I think."

"The loud man yelled, 'This is Ruby, folks! Six hundred pounds of fun to save our sorry butts,'" I continue. "I smelled old sawdust and stale cotton candy and sad animals.

"Another circus. No way was I going in there.

"The loud man and two others climbed into the truck, but I refused to budge.

"The loud man got louder. The smiling man and the

girl looked worried.

"And then Aunt Stella saved the day. Slowly she made her way up the truck's ramp. I could see the pain one of her legs was causing her.

"Nothing about her face said, 'This will be a happy place.'

"Nothing said, 'I am glad you are joining me.'

"Softly she murmured, 'Come with me now, little one. I'll do my best to care for you.'

"As we walked down the ramp, Stella and me, I heard her whisper to herself, 'I just hope my best is enough.'"

better

"Aunt Stella saved me from sadness.

"She cuddled me, loved me, promised me life could get better.

"She listened to my riddles. She answered my questions.

"And one other thing." I gaze at my dear uncle Ivan, with his shiny silver fur and gentle eyes. "Aunt Stella asked you, Uncle Ivan, to help me find a better life.

"And you did."

done

I take a deep breath.

I'm done with my story.

We sit there, Uncle Ivan and Uncle Bob and Aunt Kin-yani and me, for a long time.

Leaves chatter. Children giggle. Birds chirp.

I'm done with my story, and the world just keeps on going like it always has.

But when I look over at Uncle Ivan and Uncle Bob, I realize they're both crying.

I've watched my share of humans cry. (Mostly little kids who don't want to leave the park.) I've seen the red noses and snotty sniffles and tears rivering down cheeks.

Maybe you wonder if animals cry.

Well, we do.

Not in the same way as humans. In quieter, inside-of us ways, but you can see the hurt in our eyes if you know what to look for.

"I'm sorry," I say. "I didn't mean to make you sad." And I realize it's the second time I've said that to them.

"You are an exceptionally brave little elephant, do you know that?" Uncle Ivan says. "You've been through so much."

"You are definitely one tough cookie," Uncle Bob agrees.

Uncle Ivan looks at me fondly. "I'm glad you told us, Ruby. It's good not to keep things locked up inside," he says, and Uncle Bob groans a little.

"I know, I know, Bob," Uncle Ivan says. "I haven't wanted to talk about Stella." He pauses. "But maybe . . . I was wrong."

"It wouldn't be the first time," says Aunt Kinyani.

"Did you ever tell Stella your story?" Uncle Bob asks me.

"Yes," I say. "And she told me hers, too." I shake my head. "I remember one time at night—we used to talk all night while you guys snored away—"

"Hey, blame the big guy for that," Uncle Bob protests.

"Anyway, that night Aunt Stella talked about how she would love to be with a herd of elephants again, and I said, 'I'm your herd.'" My voice trails off. "But I knew it wasn't the same."

"Ruby! Ruby!" Someone is calling me from the visitors' area.

It's Carmen. She's holding a yellow balloon and her long hair is tied in a braid.

"Your public awaits," says Uncle Bob.

"I guess I should go," I say. "Thanks for listening. You're the best uncles ever."

"In case I don't see you, good luck tomorrow," Uncle Bob says. "You're going to rock your Tuskday. You are the one and only Ruby, and don't forget it!"

"Ruby," Uncle Ivan calls softly just as I start to leave.

"Yes, Uncle Ivan?"

"You made Stella's last days the happiest of her life." He points to me. "*You* were all the herd she ever needed."

I nod. But I'm not sure he's right.

tuskday

Even with a full moon and a cloudless night, I don't sleep at all. As soon as the keepers slide open the pavilion doors in the morning, I'm the first one outside.

It's dawn, and the dew-covered lawn sparkles like a giant green sugar cookie. (I've only had a sugar cookie once for a special treat, but it was AMAZING.) Behind me, I hear Aunt Elodie and Aunt Masika singing, "It's your Tuskday! Happy, happy Tuskday! Tusky! Tusky! We love you!"

I turn and wave my trunk, then quickly dash off before they can begin a second verse.

I realize that I'm practically running. Running from my aunts. Running from a ceremony that's just meant to . . . how did Aunt Laheli put it? To celebrate the herd. To celebrate the earth.

But herds don't last.

And the earth is a scary place sometimes.

And tusks . . . well, tusks too often mean death.

My ears are shivering and my tummy is churning and I don't know why, but I just can't do my Tuskday. Maybe tomorrow. Maybe in a month or a year.

But not today.

I check behind me. The other elephants are sauntering out of the pavilion, stretching, browsing, taking in the perfect morning air. Nobody is paying any attention to me.

I slow down, trying to calm my hammering heart, to walk nice and casual. *Just getting a little exercise. Nothing to see here, folks.*

Then I head to the faraway fence with the not-very-big hole that might just be big enough for a not-very-big elephant.

I'm a little surprised the hole hasn't been repaired. The park workers are really careful about fences and things like that. They seem to think park residents shouldn't chow down on visitors. Or on each other.

But this hole leads to a big stretch of trees and grass, and it doesn't look like an official part of the park. Parts of the fence are covered in black plastic, but through gaps I can make out lots of trucks and digging machines and piles of dirt.

The hole in the wire is about as tall as I am. There's a piece that's come loose from a metal post. It's not exactly me-sized, but it's close.

I poke my head through. No problem. Easy-peasy.

That voice in my head starts chattering. *So you get through the hole, Ruby. Then what?*

Good question, Voice.

I push a little bit more. The wire is brushing my shoulders, but I'm still okay.

Voice is waiting for an answer. "I get through the hole," I reply, "and then I hide behind the fence, and then the aunts get mad because they can't find me, and then they give up on Tuskday, and then *wah-la!* I appear and they yell at me, but I can deal with it because at least I didn't have to give a silly speech about my annoying tusks and growing up and all that."

That's a pretty bad plan, Ruby, Voice tells me, and I have to agree, but by then I've scooched another couple inches through the fence, and it turns out my tummy is a little bigger than I'd thought and uh-oh, I am extremely and unfortunately very much stuck.

It hurts to move forward. It hurts to move backward. The wire is sharp, and even with my thick elephant skin, it's poky and scratchy.

I told you so, says Voice, which is not really helpful.

Out of nowhere, I fear I'm going to cry again. It doesn't make sense. All those awful times in Africa I told Ivan and Bob about? I just dealt with them. I didn't cry. Not much, anyway.

But after seeing Jabori I cried. And now, here I am in this ridiculous position and I decide to cry?

I tell myself, *Calm down, Ruby* in my best scoldy aunt voice, and after a while, I do.

I could yell for help, but I don't want the aunts to see me like this. I don't want anyone to see me like this.

Especially Aunt Akello.

I realize that someone is calling for me. Someone nearby.

Unfortunately, it's Aunt Akello.

Of *course* it is.

Aunt Akello doesn't say anything right away. She just stands a few feet from me, taking it all in.

Which is the worst thing she can do.

I want to say, *Just go ahead and yell at me! Or at least laugh at me!* But my mouth seems to be stuck shut. It feels like I just ate a hive full of honey, bees and all.

She steps closer. She smells like fresh hay and cantaloupe, and I realize how hungry I am.

"Hello, Tusky," she says at last, in that voice of hers that's windy and cool and a tiny bit scary.

I wonder if she sounded like this when she was a little elephant.

Then I wonder if she ever even *was* a little elephant.

I force myself to speak. "Umm," I say. My voice cracks. "Hi there, Aunt Akello."

She examines the torn fence with her trunk. "Would you like to hear a riddle?" she asks.

I was expecting her to say a whole bunch of things, none of them exactly good.

But not *that*.

"Sure," I say, trying not to breathe too hard, because breathing means poky wires. "I, um, I love riddles."

"I know you do," she says, still checking the fence. "I know a lot about you, little one."

She grips a section of wire with the end of her trunk, but the fence barely moves. "All right, then," Aunt Akello says. "Here goes. What time is it when an elephant sits on a fence?"

She almost looks, I dunno, nervous? Shy? I wonder if she's ever actually told a riddle before.

The thing is, I know the answer. But should I tell her? Or should I pretend I've never heard the riddle? I wait for that bossy voice in my head to give me a clue. But it seems to have run away.

That voice is a chicken.

"Uh, I have no idea, Aunt Akello," I say. "What time is it when an elephant sits on a fence?"

She waits. At least she knows how to do that part.

"It is . . . ," she says, her eyes sparkling, "time to fix the fence!"

She looks hopeful, like she's never made anyone laugh before, and there is something so sweet and silly about her expression that I pretend to chuckle, even though of course I've heard that riddle a hundred times.

"Good one, Aunt Akello!" I say.

"I'm not much of a jokester," she admits. "But that seemed perfect, under the circumstances."

"It was for sure," I say.

"So." She points to the fence with her trunk. "What's the plan? You going somewhere?"

"Just saw the hole and got curious," I say, which is sort of not a lie, but probably still counts as Not Okay Behavior.

"Tusky," Aunt Akello says, and when she sees me make a face, she tries again. "Ruby." She yanks on a dandelion and holds it up to the sun. "I remember being afraid of my Tuskday, too."

"You?" I ask, unable to hide my surprise. It's hard to imagine Aunt Akello being afraid of anything.

"Oh, my, yes." She drops the dandelion, then reconsiders, picks it up, and eats it.

"What were you afraid of?" As soon as the words are out of my mouth, I wonder if I've asked something Not Okay.

Aunt Akello seems fine with my question. "Where to start?" she exclaims. "Everything and nothing. I had so many worries. Would I be brave enough when I grew up? Strong enough? Wise enough? Kind enough?" She gives a small laugh. "Could I, little Akello, ever lead a herd?"

"Well, here you are," I say. "Our matriarch. So I guess that worked out okay."

"True," she agrees. "But I was born, like you, in Africa.

Our herd was twenty strong, sometimes more. That's a big burden for any elephant to take upon her shoulders. Here"—she shrugs—"here it's easy. Here we just pretend to be wild. Here the keepers bring your water. There are no droughts in the park. No threats." She pauses. "Unless you count the odor coming from the water buffalo enclosure."

I belly-laugh, which is a bad idea, because my belly is stuck in a big wire fence.

"My point is," she adds, "if I'd become the matriarch of my African herd, my life would have been very different."

When we'd first met, I'd told the other elephants I was from Africa. But I hadn't realized Aunt Akello was from there, too.

Truth is, I only know little bits and pieces about my aunts and their histories. They don't talk much about the past. The only reason I know about Aunt Laheli's hurt eye and Aunt Zaina's arthritis is because I overheard them talking one afternoon.

I was not exactly eavesdropping. I was *investigating*. And elephants have excellent hearing.

It's not my fault my ears are talented.

"Are any of the other aunts from Africa?" I ask.

"No," Aunt Stella answers. "All captive-born. Circuses and roadside attractions and such." She shudders. "Not nice places. We're lucky here. Luckier than many elephants, anyway."

"Do you remember much about Africa, Aunt Akello?" I ask, because I can't help myself.

"Too much," she says. "And not enough. I suppose I pick and choose my memories."

"Uncle Ivan is like that," I say.

"Maybe that's how we manage to stay hopeful," Aunt Akello says.

"In Africa," I say softly, "there were bad people. They killed elephants because they wanted their tusks."

"When I was there I saw it, too, Ruby. I still have nightmares about it."

We fall quiet for a moment, and then I say the words out loud.

"I hate my tusks," I whisper.

Aunt Akello touches my back with her trunk, so softly she could be a moth or a morning breeze. "I know, dear one," she says. "I know."

backward

"It's true that tusks can be a burden," says Aunt Akello. "But I'm about to show you how useful they can sometimes be."

She moves closer to the fence and pushes on the wire with her left tusk. "I'm going to push this as hard as I can," she says, "and as soon as there's enough space, you back up toward me. Or head on through, if that's what you want to do."

She yanks on the edge of the wire with her left tusk. The fence is no match for her enormous strength.

But which way am I going? I listen for Voice. Nothing.

Instead I hear Aunt Zaina's words: *You can't run away from growing up. That's a race you will not win, my friend.*

I take a step forward. I take a step backward. I take

another step backward.

Looks like heading backward is the winner.

Aunt Akello checks to make sure I'm not scratched or hurt.

"I'm fine," I say. *Just a little embarrassed*, I add silently.

"Now let's you and I have a talk," she says.

"About Not Okay Behavior?" I guess.

Aunt Akello winks at me. "About tusks," she replies.

Aunt Akello leads me to a quiet spot shaded by three large pine trees. In the distance, I can hear the other elephants laughing and talking.

"It's almost time for the ceremony," says Aunt Akello. "Your aunts are quite excited."

I tug at a hunk of grass. "At least *somebody* is."

"Tusks, Ruby, are a sign that you are growing up. They're also very helpful," Aunt Akello says. "They're great for digging soil for a dirt shower, or removing tasty bark, or play-fighting, and sometimes even real fighting. Tusks are as useful to elephants as arms are to humans."

"But humans like things they are not supposed to have," I say. "My aunt Stella told me that."

"And they very much like tusks," says Aunt Akello. "See that nick in my right tusk? Poacher. Rifle. Just missed, but I got the message."

"I don't understand. It's not like I want some human's arm for a trophy. Why would someone want part of an elephant?"

"It's an excellent question," says Aunt Akello. She shakes her head. "Sometimes they make things out of the tusks. They call them 'ivory.'"

"What kinds of things?"

"They carve it up into small statues. Even little figurines of elephants, can you imagine? They make pieces for board games. They make fancy boxes. They use tiny shards to make pictures. They make piano keys—"

"What's a piano?" I ask, and I remember too late that it's rude to interrupt.

"It's a sort of big box that humans use to make silvery

sounds," Aunt Akello explains. "Of course, sometimes humans don't bother to create anything with the ivory. They just take the tusks and put them up on a wall."

"But . . . but why?"

"So they can imagine what it's like to be an elephant, I suppose." Aunt Akello strokes my back with her trunk. "After all, who wouldn't want to be one of us?"

"I know who," I say, and my voice is stormy. "The dead elephant I saw on the savanna. The one who was nothing but a pile of bones. Bones, but no tusks. Those were gone."

Aunt Akello looks at me. I have the feeling she's trying to decide just how grown up I really am.

"I've seen those bones, Ruby. My grandmother's bones. My mother's. I've seen the bones of brothers and cousins and strangers and friends." She looks up at the treetops. "Far too many times I've seen them."

"Then why should I celebrate having tusks? Why should I be excited about something people want to kill me over?" I cry.

"You're not in any danger here at the park, Ruby," says Aunt Akello gently. "You're safe with us." She gives a sharp laugh. "Safe, but not free. That's the trade-off."

"I know that," I say, although I'm not sure I really did until this moment. "But what about all the others? The ones we left behind?"

"All we can do is hope," says Aunt Akello. "I wish I had a better answer, dear one. I suppose that's one of the hardest parts of growing up."

"What do you mean?" I ask.

"Realizing that grown-ups don't have all the answers. Realizing that the answers may have to come from you."

a question

Aunt Akello begins walking back toward the large pond where the others are waiting, and I join her. What else can I do? Where else can I go?

"It looks like your herd is ready for you," says Aunt Akello, and I notice that the group is gathered together, watching us approach.

"My herd," I say, feeling the weight of those words. "Aunt Stella wanted to be with a herd one more time. I wish . . . I wish she could be here today."

"Perhaps she will be." Aunt Akello looks at me with a mysterious smile. "In some way."

When we get a bit closer, Aunt Elodie and Aunt Masika begin singing. "It's your Tuskday! Happy, happy Tuskday! Tusky! Tusky! We love you!"

Aunt Laheli and Aunt Zaina are standing on either side of them. When the second verse begins, even they join in, although Aunt Zaina is not-so-secretly rolling her eyes.

By the time they're done with the third verse, Aunt Akello and I have arrived. The aunts step aside to reveal a large circle they've made out of sticks, grasses, leaves, and flowers. The circle is right next to Aunt Zaina's shoulder boulder so that she has a convenient place to lean.

Aunt Akello throws up her trunk and makes a glorious trumpeting sound. "Attention, Herd of the Park!" she proclaims. "Today we celebrate the Tuskday of our beloved herdmate, Ruby of the Park! Please take your positions."

The aunts move to four points on the circle, standing along the outside edge. Aunt Zaina takes the spot next to her shoulder boulder. I have to admit the circle is really quite beautiful, especially the carefully placed dandelion blossoms.

Between Aunt Zaina and Aunt Laheli I notice a smooth stick, stripped of leaves, planted upright in the dirt. It's a little bit curved and about the same length as one of Aunt Akello's tusks.

Aunt Akello moves to the center of the circle, carefully stepping over the sticks and flowers. "Ruby of the Park," she commands, "please enter the Heart of the Herd."

I gulp. I take a step. I guess I'm doing this, after all.

But everyone looks so serious! For some reason, I think of Uncle Bob and decide I'll try to lighten the mood a little.

"Okay," I say, "but first I have a question. How come this isn't called 'Tusksday,' with an extra S in the middle? I mean, we have two tusks, right?"

Instantly I'm worried that I've just performed an extremely Not Okay Behavior. But when everyone laughs, even Aunt Akello, I relax.

"It's simple," she answers. "'Tusksday' is just too hard to say."

a moment of silence

I step into the circle and stand beside Aunt Akello.

"Let us begin, as we always begin," Aunt Akello says in her soft voice, "with a moment of silence for our ancestors."

All the aunts raise their trunks skyward, eyes closed, so I do the same.

In the quiet, the world seems to come alive with noise: humans and animals, birds and bugs, honking cars and growling trucks. The sun pours down on my back and my trunk is getting a little tired, so I open one eye to see if we're done yet. Even Aunt Zaina still has her trunk raised, although it's wobbling a bit, so I close my eye and keep listening.

It's sort of beautiful, I realize, the world's sounds, all mixed together to make a strange melody.

At last Aunt Akello breaks the spell. "You may lower your trunks and rejoin the present," she says, and everyone relaxes. "Today we gather to acknowledge the Tuskday of our youngest herdmate, Ruby of the Park. In attendance we have Zaina of the Park, Laheli of the Park, Masika of the Park, and Elodie of the Park." Each aunt bows her head low when she hears her name mentioned. "I am Akello of the Park and Matriarch of the Park Herd."

With her trunk, Aunt Akello points to the stick planted in the ground between Aunt Zaina and Aunt Laheli. "Let us now honor the presence of Stella of—" She hesitates and turns to me. "Where was Stella's last home?" she asks.

I'm confused. Why is she bringing up Aunt Stella? "The Exit 8 Big Top Mall and Video Arcade," I answer. "But it wasn't much of a home."

Aunt Akello frowns. "That will never do." She thinks for a moment. "Let us now honor the presence of Stella of the African Savanna."

She walks over to the stick and softly touches the top of it with her trunk. The other aunts do the same, trunk upon trunk upon trunk upon trunk. Aunt Akello signals me to join them.

I place my trunk on top of the others. "The ones we love," says Aunt Akello, "live forever in our hearts."

I am trying hard not to cry, but my words come out in gulps and sobs. "I wonder if . . . ," I begin, but I have to stop, and the aunts, all of them, move their trunks from the stick to me, and they are patting me and stroking me and soothing me with so much love I can't imagine why I deserve it all.

Finally I manage to find my voice. "I wonder if maybe, along with 'Stella of the African Savanna,' we could also call her 'Stella of the Park,' like the rest of us? She really wanted to be with a herd again and . . . well, I can't think of a better one than this."

Aunt Akello nods. "'Stella of the Park' it is."

Aunt Akello returns to the center of the circle, and I follow her. The other aunts take their positions at the edge.

"Now that we have all assembled," says Aunt Akello, "we shall recite the Four Lodestars. A lodestar, as some of you know, is a guiding star on a dark evening, a beacon to help us navigate the terrain of our lives. Wild elephants spend much of their time traveling at night. For them, the stars are as necessary as air. The same is true for us, though we no longer move through the world like our wild kin."

She clears her throat and begins, in a loud, clear voice: "We are not our best selves without kindness."

The other aunts respond, all speaking together: "An elephant without kindness is not an elephant."

"We are not our best selves without wonder," says Aunt Akello.

"An elephant without wonder is not an elephant," the aunts respond.

"We are not our best selves without courage," says Aunt Akello.

"An elephant without courage is not an elephant," the aunts respond.

"We are not our best selves without gratitude," says Aunt Akello.

"An elephant without gratitude is not an elephant," the aunts respond.

Aunt Akello pauses and looks down at me. "To be born elephant is a great gift. To be part of a herd is to be part of this beautiful world. But make no mistake: that does not mean you should blindly follow your herd. It *does* mean we must strive for connection despite our differences." She smiles. "And that is why we say, 'An elephant alone is not an elephant.' Because, dear Ruby of the Park, we all need each other."

Aunt Akello takes a few steps back, and I am by myself in the center of the circle. "And now the time has come for you to tell us what Tuskday means to you. Are you prepared?"

No! I think, and I realize I'm trembling. But I locate my voice and squeak, "I hope so."

another riddle

The aunts gaze at me hopefully, and it feels a little like the nights when Aunt Stella used to ask me her two questions. I don't want to let them all down. But I'm still not sure how to answer.

I want to say that Tuskday means worry and lost sleep and getting stuck in a fence. I want to say that tusks mean very little when you're a captive elephant, and they mean too much—even death—when you're wild.

I look at each of my aunts: grumpy Aunt Zaina, and silly Aunt Elodie, and the singing pair of Aunt Laheli and Aunt Masika. Then I turn to Aunt Akello, huge and wise and always and probably forever just a little bit scary. They're all smiling at me, their eyes wide with anticipation, just the way Aunt Stella's used to be.

My little herd.

"There's this, um . . ." I pause, because apparently I've forgotten how to breathe. "There's this riddle—you all know how much I like riddles, right? Well, there's this riddle, and I don't know why, but it just popped into my head and it kind of says what I think Tuskday is all about. So here goes."

I wait a moment, because it's good to build suspense.

"Ready?" I ask, and they all nod.

"I am a ship that's built to ride the greatest waves," I say. "I'm not built with hammers. I'm built with hearts. What kind of ship am I?"

I wait again. You can't rush a good riddle.

"Anyone?" I say, but they all shake their heads.

"I'll give you a hint," I say. "We all have it." More confused looks. "What kind of ship am I?" I ask again.

I can't stand it, so I shout the answer: "I'm *friend*ship!"

The aunts smile and laugh, and Aunt Elodie pounds her trunk on the ground. "Anyway," I say, "I guess what I mean is maybe getting tusks and growing up isn't all bad. I kind of like the idea of being a good friend and taking care of others the way everybody's always taken care of me." I cast a sly glance at Aunt Akello. "Also, once you've had your Tuskday, you get an hour more of mudfun every day, right?"

Aunt Akello's not buying it. "Before we end the ceremony, Ruby of the Park, from now on there's something you must do. It's a sort of daily checkup of your heart and your mind. It's both extremely simple and hugely difficult."

"Wait!" I say. "Are you saying we're almost done and I passed the test?"

"There was never any doubt of that, dear one," says Aunt Akello.

"Can we wrap this up soon?" Aunt Zaina grumbles. "My feet are killing me."

"Every day," says Aunt Akello, "pick a quiet time and ask yourself these two questions. 'What gifts did the world give you today? What gifts did you give the world?'"

"No problem!" I say, practically skipping with relief. "*Now* are we done?"

"Not so fast. Think about what that means for a moment. Say the words out loud."

"What gifts did the world give you today? What gifts did you give the world?" I say. "I guess that first one means what made me happy or excited or curious today, and the other one means did I do something, you know, nice for somebody or something—" I stop cold, because all at once I'm hearing Aunt Stella's voice, as if she's standing right there next to me, asking me, with different words, the same two questions: *What amazed you today, little Ruby? What made you proud?*

I'd never lost her. She was here with me all along.

I walk over to the stick in the ground and pat it gently with my trunk. "Don't worry, Aunt Stella," I whisper. "You taught me well. I got this."

Before dinner, I stop by Canine Corner to see Uncle Bob and Uncle Ivan. Aunt Kinyani is there, too, munching on a piece of pineapple.

"So how was the big Tuskday ceremony?" Uncle Bob asks.

"You know," I say, "it was actually pretty great. They even had a special place set aside for—" I cut myself short, but Uncle Ivan finishes my sentence.

"For Stella," he says.

"How did you know that, Uncle Ivan?" I ask.

He shrugs. "Akello came up this way yesterday. She was worried about you, and we talked about Stella a little."

I smile at him. It's pretty great when you know that others are looking out for you. I hope I get the chance to do that someday soon.

"I even told a riddle," I say. "The one about friendship."

"Hammers and hearts?" says Uncle Bob. "A classic."

"You know another classic?" Uncle Ivan asks, as he cuddles next to Aunt Kinyani. "That riddle Stella loved. Something about an elephant crossing the road?"

I'm surprised to hear him bring up Aunt Stella again, but he looks happy. "Why did the elephant cross the road?" I say.

"Yeah, that one," Uncle Ivan says. "It always made her laugh."

"Because the chicken retired," I say, and we all smile.

"She loved that one about the footprints in the butter, too," Uncle Bob says fondly.

"How can you tell if an elephant's been in the refrigerator?" I say. "That was one of her favorites."

We keep thinking of more elephant riddles, and before we know it, we are sharing Aunt Stella stories until the sun begins to set.

It's late, and all the aunts are dozing here and there in the pavilion. Mwezi is big and yellow, like a glowing dandelion, and the only sound is Aunt Zaina's snoring.

I feel the same, now that my Tuskday is over. And I feel different, too. How can that be?

It's a mystery.

But that's okay. I like mysteries. They're like riddles, without the giggling.

I think of the questions I am supposed to ask myself from now on. *What gifts did the world give you today? What gifts did you give to the world?*

Thanks to Aunt Stella, I've had plenty of practice for this.

The second one is pretty easy.

I tried my best to be brave today, even when I was afraid. After the ceremony, I thanked all my aunts, especially Aunt Akello, for their hard work on my Tuskday, and I told everyone how much I love them.

But that first one? The one about the gifts the world gave me today?

I don't even know where to start.

I may be the littlest elephant.

But I'm also the luckiest.

author's note

In a perfect world, elephants would roam free in their natural habitats, peacefully coexisting with humans. Unfortunately, we don't live in a perfect world, and many scientists agree that as climate change continues to shrink available resources, we need well-run, accredited sanctuaries and zoos. They also agree that providing ample open space and the company of other elephants is vitally important in such situations. Sadly, often because of budgetary constraints, that is not always the case.

Carefully managed ecotourism is another way to protect existing elephant populations. It can deter poaching, benefit local communities, and allow elephants to live their best lives.

Despite the efforts of dedicated conservationists, many elephants continue to suffer in horrible conditions, often in roadside zoos or traveling circuses. Far too many members of this highly intelligent and social species live alone, unable to move more than a few yards at a time. If you encounter such a place, an important action you can take is to walk away. Don't give them your money.

Do let them know that these beautiful creatures deserve far better.

Although there have been encouraging efforts to ban the international ivory trade in the past decade, elephant poaching continues to be a devastating problem. One shocking result of endless years of poaching is the evolution of elephants with smaller tusks, or no tusks at all, in some heavily hunted populations.

If you're interested in elephant behavior, I highly recommend the elephant ethogram at the website of ElephantVoices, an organization cofounded by the renowned elephant researcher Joyce Poole (www.elephantvoices .org/elephant-ethogram/introduction.html). An ethogram is a comprehensive catalog of behaviors, and this one features wonderfully detailed videos. You can even see floppy-running, one of Ruby's favorite pastimes!

The Sheldrick Wildlife Trust, one of Africa's oldest wildlife charities, is doing remarkable work rescuing and rehabilitating orphaned elephants. Their website features fascinating, heartbreaking, and hopeful stories about the many elephant, rhino, and giraffe babies whose lives they have saved, and their incredible efforts helped inspire Ruby's story. www.sheldrickwildlifetrust.org/faqs.

The phrase "An elephant alone is not an elephant"

was inspired by a passage I came across many years ago while doing research for *The One and Only Ivan*. While I'd love to credit the source, despite my best efforts, I can't seem to locate it. The point, of course, is that separating a member of a species from others of its own kind is inherently cruel. Truer words have never been spoken— even if I can't recall who said them.

acknowledgments

When a baby elephant joins the world, it takes an entire herd to ensure that she thrives and becomes all she's meant to be. The same holds true for a newborn story. Few readers realize just how many dedicated professionals are involved in a book's upbringing. It's a whole lot of work. Stories can be cranky, stubborn, and whiny (and so can authors.)

I'm truly grateful to the many "sentinels" at Harper-Collins who helped shepherd *The One and Only Ruby* from messy manuscript to the gorgeous book you now hold in your hands, including: Sarah Homer, Mark Rifkin, Shona McCarthy, Valerie Shea, Catherine Mallette, Amy Ryan, Vanessa Nuttry, Vaishali Nayak, Nellie Kurtzman, Ann Dye, Jenn Corcoran, Patty Rosati, Mimi Rankin, Christina Carpino, Caitlin Garing, Almeda Beynon, and the incredible HC sales team.

Special thanks go to my brilliant agent, Elena Giovinazzo, at Pippin Properties; to Patricia Castelao, whose illustrations make Ruby's story come alive; and, of course, to Tara Weikum, my remarkable editor.

Finally, endless gratitude to my friends and family, and to the wonderful readers who asked to see how our little Ruby has been doing.

I think she's going to be just fine.

See where Ivan and Bob's story began
in this sneak peek at the Newbery Award–winning
and *New York Times* bestselling modern classic,
The One and Only Ivan!

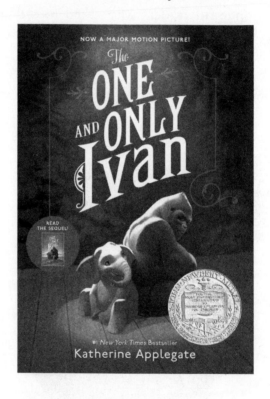

hello

I am Ivan. I am a gorilla.

It's not as easy as it looks.

names

People call me the Freeway Gorilla. The Ape at Exit 8. The One and Only Ivan, Mighty Silverback.

The names are mine, but they're not me. I am Ivan, just Ivan, only Ivan.

Humans waste words. They toss them like banana peels and leave them to rot.

Everyone knows the peels are the best part.

I suppose you think gorillas can't understand you. Of course, you also probably think we can't walk upright.

Try knuckle walking for an hour. You tell me: Which way is more fun?

patience

I've learned to understand human words over the years, but understanding human speech is not the same as understanding humans.

Humans speak too much. They chatter like chimps, crowding the world with their noise even when they have nothing to say.

It took me some time to recognize all those human sounds, to weave words into things. But I was patient.

Patient is a useful way to be when you're an ape.

Gorillas are as patient as stones. Humans, not so much.

how I look

I used to be a wild gorilla, and I still look the part.

I have a gorilla's shy gaze, a gorilla's sly smile. I wear a snowy saddle of fur, the uniform of a silverback. When the sun warms my back, I cast a gorilla's majestic shadow.

In my size humans see a test of themselves. They hear fighting words on the wind, when all I'm thinking is how the late-day sun reminds me of a ripe nectarine.

I'm mightier than any human, four hundred pounds of pure power. My body looks made for battle. My arms, outstretched, span taller than the tallest human.

My family tree spreads wide as well. I am a great ape, and you are a great ape, and so are chimpanzees and orangutans and bonobos, all of us distant and distrustful cousins.

I know this is troubling.

I too find it hard to believe there is a connection across time and space, linking me to a race of ill-mannered clowns.

Chimps. There's no excuse for them.

the exit 8 big top mall
and video arcade

I live in a human habitat called the Exit 8 Big Top Mall and Video Arcade. We are conveniently located off I-95, with shows at two, four, and seven, 365 days a year.

Mack says that when he answers the trilling telephone.

Mack works here at the mall. He is the boss.

I work here too. I am the gorilla.

At the Big Top Mall, a creaky-music carousel spins all day, and monkeys and parrots live amid the merchants. In the middle of the mall is a ring with benches where humans can sit on their rumps while they eat soft pretzels. The floor is covered with sawdust made of dead trees.

My domain is at one end of the ring. I live here because I am too much gorilla and not enough human.

Stella's domain is next to mine. Stella is an elephant. She and Bob, who is a dog, are my dearest friends.

At present, I do not have any gorilla friends.

My domain is made of thick glass and rusty metal and rough cement. Stella's domain is made of metal bars. The sun bears' domain is wood; the parrots' is wire mesh.

Three of my walls are glass. One of them is cracked, and a small piece, about the size of my hand, is missing from its bottom corner. I made the hole with a baseball bat Mack gave me for my sixth birthday. After that he took the bat away, but he let me keep the baseball that came with it.

A jungle scene is painted on one of my domain walls. It has a waterfall without water and flowers without scent and trees without roots. I didn't paint it, but I enjoy the way the shapes flow across my wall, even if it isn't much of a jungle.

I am lucky my domain has three windowed walls. I can see the whole mall and a bit of the world beyond: the frantic pinball machines, the pink billows of cotton candy, the vast and treeless parking lot.

Beyond the lot is a freeway where cars stampede without end. A giant sign at its edge beckons them to stop and rest like gazelles at a watering hole.

The sign is faded, the colors bleeding, but I know what it says. Mack read its words aloud one day: "COME TO THE EXIT 8 BIG TOP MALL AND VIDEO ARCADE, HOME OF THE ONE AND ONLY IVAN, MIGHTY SILVERBACK!"

Sadly, I cannot read, although I wish I could. Reading stories would make a fine way to fill my empty hours.

Once, however, I was able to enjoy a book left in my domain by one of my keepers.

It tasted like termite.

The freeway billboard has a drawing of Mack in his clown clothes and Stella on her hind legs and an angry animal with fierce eyes and unkempt hair.

That animal is supposed to be me, but the artist made a mistake. I am never angry.

Anger is precious. A silverback uses anger to maintain order and warn his troop of danger. When my father beat his chest, it was to say, *Beware, listen, I am in charge. I am angry to protect you, because that is what I was born to do.*

Here in my domain, there is no one to protect.